NINEVEH:
A CONFLICT OVER WATER

papi kymone freeman

DEDICATED TO

All the children we have lost
and to Damu Smith
Architect of the
Environmental Justice Movement

TABLE OF CONTENTS

PROLOGUE

I see in the near future a crisis approaching that unnerves me to tremble for the safety of my country. Corporations have been enthroned and an era of corruption in high places will follow and the money power of the country will endeavor to prolong its reign by working upon the prejudices of the people until all wealth is aggregated in a few hands and the Republic is destroyed.

Abraham Lincoln

16th President of the U.S.

November 21st 1864

"You are not a drop in the ocean.
You are the entire ocean in one drop"

—Rumi

CHAPTER 1

THE NATURE OF THE PROBLEM

Believe it or not. Nineveh is not in the distant future. Nor is it in a land far, far away. Brutal water wars have long taken the form of low intensity conflicts that didn't even make the news for decades. Whoever controls the land controls how the history is told on that land. Veolia, which was once the world's largest privately owned public utility company, also owned major broadcast media companies. That's why when the notoriously bloody war criminal George Bush bought hundreds of thousands of acres in the South American country of Paraguay to gain access to the Guarani Aquifer that contained enough fresh water to fully sustain the world's population for 200 years the corporate media didn't say a word. No one cared where our water came from or where it went. Continuing the insane position that resulted in no one in power taking responsibility for the health of the planet. The unjust world we live in, its divisions, disparities, never ending wars and conflicts for profit, its widening gap between the rich and the poor, its seemingly inexplicable outbursts of violence are shaped far less by what we celebrate and mythologize than by the painful events and stories about power and origin we all try to forget.

At the time this story begins, the entire world is feeling the impact of human greed on the environment. It's like they're taking machine guns mowing down the lives of indigenous people. The prospect that two-thirds of the world's population would have no access to fresh drinking water by 2025 provoked the initial confrontation in the world wide battle for control of the planet's most basic resource. In the entire history of civilization water has always been the principal determining factor if they were successful or not. The epoch of climate change has now surpassed the global warming tipping point and put the entire planet on a respirator where the Amazon Rainforest has been destroyed, rivers are polluted or dried up, and oceans are acidic. Bees, the number one pollinators, are nearly extinct and the melting polar ice caps have caused cessation ocean levels to rise drastically. Entire cities have now been submerged, whereas new ones have emerged. Wet areas got wetter and dry areas got drier. The rich got richer and the poor got poorer. And they all met in Nineveh.

As a result, life is harder than ever before with paper currency rendered worthless and only crypto currency or gold remaining as the standard for bartering recorded on a purchase card. Nearly everything requires water to make which is the tide that raises the prices for everything. Nowhere is this fact more apparent than in the extreme food prices. Therefore, skinny people comprise the underclass and obesity is now a mark of beauty and power possessed only by the elite.

As a survival technique, diets themselves have changed drastically. Meat production accounts for nearly 60% of all greenhouse gases in the old world. In this new world order of crisis it is reserved only for the elite. To avoid starvation, the new lumpen proletariats of Nineveh, have taken to farming snakehead fish in abandoned pools in secret locations. The snakehead fish is able to become a staple food source because a female can lay up to fifteen thousand eggs up to five times a year! In addition, adult snakehead fish can feed on rats of which an unlimited supply to be found in Nineveh, so that it also serves as an effective method for rodent extermination. Plus the snakehead fish flesh tasted a lot better than the notion of actually eating rats. Of course, rabbits are a different kind of rodent altogether that also taste better and their reputation of reproduction prowess precedes them.

One such morbidly obese person of excess that is obviously used to taking advantage of opportunities that misery and poverty provides by exploiting them for his own sexual perversion is cruising Nineveh's Southside streets, where the feeling of death and ruin is felt strongest. He is scouring the streets for someone hungry or thirsty enough, or simply tired of rations of rabbit and fish, to satisfy his lustful cravings. He spots Evolon walking alone boldly down the street like she has diamonds on the soles of her shoes. She is a tall, dark, rebelliously beautiful young woman with long regal locks. Her dark eyes shine like polished black rifles on arsenal walls. She is powerfully built and fashionably dressed completely embodying the spirit of Dahomey Amazon warriors that knew it takes more than bullets to kill a man.

Undeterred, he pulls over with an air of superiority and slows down his silent hydrogen fuel cell car to match the speed of her stroll. He rolls down the passenger window halfway with a condescending and ridiculous smile on his ugly face with pearly white teeth. Evolon pretends she doesn't notice and ignores the scene as she is approached by one of the politest citizens Nineveh has to offer. He speeds up, parks the car ahead of her to cut her off and gets out. He puts his face mask on to try to mediate the stench of urine stained streets that sometimes even made breathing unbearable. As he gets out of the car, he has carelessly left a water bottle in plain view in the front seat. It has not gone unnoticed. Before his lewd comments commence as he approaches her, the sounds of breaking glass are heard as a brick goes through his window. A thirsty child makes off with the bottle of water.

It is fruitless for the fat man to try to give chase, so he shrugs it off and eyes Evolon. "Hey baby, don't worry about that. It's a lot more where that came from. How would you like to join me for a steak dinner?" he says.

"Do I look hungry to you?" is her curt reply.

In true toxic form he grabs his genitals and slowly eyes her full figure up and down. "No, but you sure do make my mouth water. So how about a little meat and potatoes, huh?" he hisses.

Evelyn says, "Sorry." She tries to continue on her way, but her path is again blocked by his large frame.

"Come on, everyone loves a good steak dinner, don't they?" as he grabs her hand. She immediately snatches her hand back.

"Look, it takes five times the amount of water to get ten grams of protein from cloned beef than from natural lentils. So, I am a vegetarian and as right as rain. I don't eat that shit or with shit" she declares in defiance.

The land mammal that drinks the most water per pound of its body weight is the cow. An adult cow used for milk production can drink up to 100 gallons of water a day. In the case of lactating mothers, this number can even increase two-fold, especially during hot summer months. Beef production itself causes greenhouse emissions. Through the agricultural production process and through land-use change. Cows emit methane, a potent greenhouse gas, as they digest grasses and plants. Not to mention, but most importantly, beef production requires increasing quantities of land. New pastureland is often created by cutting down trees, which releases more carbon dioxide that is otherwise stored in forests.

"Suit yourself bitch. I can get a piece of ass for a goddamn cheeseburger, but I am not above taking it." He violently grabs her which could have been a fatal mistake under normal circumstances.

Fortunately for this poor excuse for a man, Evolon is too close to the entrance of a Resisters stronghold and doesn't want to jeopardize revealing their secret location. Rather, Evolon calmly looks him in the eyes, despite his crude violation, while pulling a gun from her long coat. She puts it against his testicles so hard that the pressure alone is enough to make his eyes water rather than his mouth and bring him excruciating pain. He hears her pull the slide back loading the chamber, and is momentarily frozen by fear. Her eyes never leave his. "Would you like anything else with that?" she says courteously while removing his wallet from his back pocket. He panics like a deer caught in headlights, and finally takes off running as fast as a fat man's legs can carry him. Which is very significant as nobody runs in Nineveh if they can help it. This conserves water because the lungs need to be kept moist for smooth breathing. Less breathing means less drinking. Then he jumps in his car with the broken glass on his seat and speeds off burning rubber and cursing all the while shattered shards of glass cut into his fat ass. Evolon takes his purchase card out and holds the wallet up in the air. She then screams "Hey, you forgot your change!"

This is Nineveh. Not since the Berlin Conference have so many borders been created or destroyed. This dire paradigm shift has resulted in the forced migrations of billions of Water Refugees worldwide searching for higher ground. Many millions of them, with the promise of guaranteed water rations, settle in the new mega city-state of Nineveh which has emerged as the new preeminent oasis. It is the largest and wealthiest city in the world with a fresh water source and near stable food supply. But you wouldn't know that looking from the ground up. It is also home of the greatest disparity in wealth and resources the planet has ever seen. Sometimes during a crisis, incentives and financial motivations may change, but never does it ever eradicate the existence of economic exploitation. It may forcibly lead to new cooperative behavior amongst some of the proletariat, but does not create more humanity amongst any of the elite in power.

In a place with only six hours of sunlight, a negative side effect of geoengineering in a failed effort to stabilize rising global temperatures via solar radiation management, you cannot expect too many bright hopes, ideas or flowers. Faced with inertia at the leadership level and a grossly apathetic world population that was initially not fully aware of the scale of the problem, "Blue Gold" that crucial life producing element that distinguishes earth from the 8 other planets in our solar system has become the standard that all wealth is now measured by.

All of which is completely controlled by the horrific Global Water corporation. Its headquarters are located in Nineveh, the new Rome. One contract for essential services is a cash cow and Global Water now has them all. Just like the Great Migration of people in America from the South looking for better resources and opportunities only to find the inescapable stench of oppression everywhere and the migrant farmworkers heading west for farm labor jobs have all discovered their dreams were illusory. The Water Refugees that fled areas ravished by water scarcity and food insecurity flooded Nineveh with the promise of more water with guaranteed rations only to receive a mere five liters per person which is grossly insufficient. They are forced to wait in line for hours to receive those limited rations at guarded stations for water and staple food. The demand for water exceeds the amount made available to the public and the available surplus is priced well beyond the level of affordability of the masses. Despite a universal basic income, which too proves to be inadequate, this has resulted in the highest crime rate in recorded history with tacit, sanctioned murder. The suicide rate surpasses that of the servicemen of the greatest military power before that empire too fell. The level of corruption and violence found here trumps that of any world power ever known.

Diametrically opposed to humanity, these conditions have produced the perfect vortex of criminal and political violence. They say when poverty knocks at the door, love goes out the window. Well, with food and water more expensive than rent, it may very well have jumped screaming to its untimely death. In this new world, many have lost all internal connectedness to life. These are tough times. These are times that will make weak men moan and strong men cry. No one without a gun or a milliliter of sense would be caught out on the street alone after dark and the only thing more dangerous on the Southside of Nineveh than being surrounded by some of the worst figments of your deepest, darkest nightmares, are the sadistic Security Forces.

We hold these truths to be self-evident, that all men are created equal, that they are endowed by their Creator with certain inalienable Rights, that among these are Life, Liberty, and the pursuit of Happiness.

If a man doesn't have food or water, he has neither life nor liberty nor the possibility for the pursuit of happiness. He merely exists. Many of the survivors of this subhuman condition had ceased to live a long time ago and accepted their fate. They merely exist. Laboring like worker ants during the short days and scurrying like cockroaches with the lights on during the long nights. These nostalgic failures were lulled into an apathetic coma, but even when awake they recognized the simple truth. They are already dead.

Only left to breathe and wait for the bullet. But the relatively few know that after every long dark night comes a glorious morning. That even if you cut all the flowers, you can't stop spring from coming.

This disturbing trend in the water sector began at the turn of the 21st century and quickly accelerated worldwide. But betrayal wears a pretty face. Some say it all began in 1863 when Perrier became the first bottled water product to reach the market. They dominated for over a century until Perrier's reputation for purity suffered a blow in 1990 when toxic benzene was found in several bottles. In desperation, Perrier claimed it was an isolated incident of a worker having made a mistake in filtering and that the spring itself was unpolluted. Nevertheless, this scandalous international incident was as corrupt as the House of Gucci and resulted in the worldwide withdrawal of the product. Over 160 million bottles were removed from market. It was finally purchased by Nestle, the world's leading food and drink company at the time, that was rumored to have been the actual culprit planting benzene, the cancer causing carcinogen, into the water supply in the first place to force the sale of disaster capitalism.

Some even say it began during the fall of the American Apartheid system. When free public water fountains were no longer legal symbols of the

Apartheid system it marked the end of the notion of free water. The eroding public confidence in the quality of the free water supply delivery system coincided with the disappearance of public water fountains and the rise of new commodified products replaced them.

Nevertheless, after this corporate takeover, the new vicious water barons and elitist multibillionaires bought up water all over the world at an unprecedented pace financed by the iniquitous International Monetary Fund and the World Bank under the direction of the heinous Bilderberg Group. Other Mega-banks and investing powerhouses followed suit and bought thousands of acres of land with aquifers, lakes, water rights, water utilities and shares in water engineering and technology companies all over the world.

The second disturbing trend is that while the new water barons were buying up water all over the world, governments were moving fast to limit citizens' ability to become self-sufficient. Nefarious corporations like Monsanto sought to control food production by promoting biotech terminator technology with seedless commodities. This resulted in hundreds of thousands of farmers committing suicide to escape the economic slavery of corporate dependency that reduced them to modern day sharecroppers with no ownership of the fruits of their labor by constantly having to purchase sterile seeds that will never reproduce. The masses barely noticed the advent of seedless fruit and the disappearance of seeded fruit available on the market.

It was a New World Order in which multibillionaires and elitist banks could own aquifers and lakes, but ordinary citizens cannot even collect rainwater and snow runoff in their own backyards and private lands. In a rapid move into the water sector, the powers that be, bought up not only water rights and water-treatment technologies, but also moved to privatize public water utilities and infrastructure to control the world's most crucial resource. The false promise of privatization was that the free market would be better stewards than government owned municipal water services. The trickle down effect resulted in cost being the key factor rather than quality of service or quantity of the product. Water become the most valuable commodity rather than the most important human right. By 2008 water was declared the "new oil of the 21st century" as the new conflict resource. It was predicted to even eclipse Agriculture and Precious Metals for those investors who knew how to play the infrastructure boom and were set to reap huge rewards. This gave rise to the Global Water Corporation that successfully competed with the largest water barons in the world when they discovered an unknown fresh water source. All they needed to profit from the defining crisis of the 21st Century: Water Scarcity.

This all set the stage for the apocalyptic Water Crisis of 2029. Paradoxically fueled by an Oil Crisis as the result of a Civil War in America, the largest consumer of oil, and another Civil War in Saudia Arabia, the largest producer of oil, combined to disrupt the world's supply chain and mark the decline of those empires. This practically ended commercial flights as airlines were being replaced by Hyperloop vehicles able to maintain flight speeds on the ground in air sealed enclosed tubes but weren't yet able to cross oceans with construction costs mired in debate between nations and served to only further divide the world. With this new demand of a dwindling resource, the tenements of unrestrained capitalism saw a lucrative opportunity to maximize the profits of the remaining fossil fuel industry by supplying hydraulic fracturing as it generated massive demands for water and water services. Each oil well developed requires 3 to 5 million gallons of water, and 80% of this water cannot be reused because it's three to 10 times saltier than seawater. Greed begets greed and water-rights owners sold water to fracking companies instead of to farmers because water for fracking could be sold for as much as $3,000 per cubic meter instead of only $50 per cubic meter to farmers. The resulting food shortages were further exacerbated by the displaced farmers who fled to the emerging cities due to this corrupt, untenable economic reality.

Areas that were once the world's breadbasket, became dust bowls during this calamitous water shortage combined with the decimation of the bee population further devastated the ability to even grow food. A drought of biblical proportions swept over the four corners of the Earth from the Inter-Tropical Convergence Zone to Nineveh and its surrounding lush provinces that were now incapable of producing their largest export. But drought could be mitigated by irrigation. So an irrigation system building plan was proposed. It was part of an ambitious project, the biggest at the time in the world that was to include the southern and eastern provinces. Had it been completed, it would have watered over 500,000 hectares of the surrounding plains and possibly mitigated the water crisis.

Instead, the government and it's corrupt leadership decided to scrap that plan deeming it too much of a socialist program framework and determined to rather address Nineveh's dilapidated water sector by selfishly imposing the proposed need of an immediate investment in a dam that would better enable them to provide a broader water distribution, but in reality it just made it easier to concentrate and control the limited supply and increase the demand. Cheaply constructed on soluble gypsum beds, meaning the subsoil would need constant grouting to keep the dam from sinking and disintegrating which is exactly what happened eventually and triggered a massive tidal wave displacing millions of Water Refugees again and killing thousands downstream.

Inadequate regulation of pollution and sewage, and chronic neglect and mismanagement of water infrastructure, had caused the quality of Nineveh's waterways to deteriorate long before the current crisis. Depriving the people in the governorate of their right to safe drinking water. Thousands of survivors began pouring into hospitals suffering from rashes, abdominal pain, vomiting, and diarrhea at pandemic levels, overwhelming staff and available stocks of medicine.

The government's Health Directorate never identified water contamination as a likely cause or called on people to boil all water before drinking or cooking with it. This resulted in an epidemic of cholera and other preventable diseases. Hundreds of residents stormed the Health Directorate to protest the poor health services afforded to those who had fallen ill. Yet after all these crises authorities failed to properly address the underlying causes or establish procedures to protect residents before the next crisis arose. The sadistic Security Forces even opened fire on the protesters in an effort to maintain law and order. Moreover, authorities continued to allow and turn a blind eye to activities that polluted Nineveh's water resources and lead to a further decline in water despite the health risks to residents.

These failures combined violated residents' right to water, sanitation, health, information, and environment guaranteed under international law. Nineveh was now plagued like the rest of the remaining world above sea level by mass unemployment, minimal public utilities, and untenable economic conditions.

The high cost of clean water fell hardest on the poorest residents and made them particularly vulnerable to unsafe tap water. One third of Nineveh lived in informal housing spread throughout the governorate that excluded the formal water and sanitation network, making them among the most water insecure. As a result, some resorted to illegally tapping into the water network where pipes ran near their homes. Water theft from illegal water hydrants could generate more money in one day than most made in a year.

Unsurprisingly, waterways were raided, but unfortunately replete with contaminants from human, animal, industrial and agricultural waste like the last city at the bottom of a long polluted river. Needlessly to say, these ill informed actions negatively impacted the already deteriorating quality of water for all residents who couldn't afford to pay. High temperatures and increased sunlight in the summer months created the perfect storm for algal blooms with Cyanobacteria that produced cyanotoxins which are among the most powerful natural poisons known to man. Nineveh was literally being poisoned by the remaining water and sealed it's fate of despair. It was under the threat of falling as quickly as it had risen. As the failed state had proven itself incapable or unwilling to provide residents with adequate safe, fresh water, it gave rise to the world's ultimate fascist private water sector in a proliferated grab to consolidate power in the crisis driven disaster capitalism with promises.

With nearly two thirds of the world's population facing water shortages, the Global Water Corporation promised clean water, guaranteed free rations, safer Security Forces and provided a new mobile water distribution system model since the public had no confidence in the previously established channels of government water lines that were tainted by lead. Water scarcity presented a growing risk for businesses and communities around the world and presented high-profile investors looking to capitalize on the newly launched lucrative water future contracts in the oasis of the New World.

Water futures joined the likes of gold and replaced the depleted oil reserves as traded stocks. The Water Market exploded with the demand for the life-sustaining natural resource continuing to climb as supply fell amid an increasingly uncertain climate environment. The index was driven by the volume-weighted average of the transaction prices in the largest and most actively traded water markets. Not knowing what is about to happen next throughly unsettles the ordinary, but experienced investors could now take a stake in this most essential liquid, a development that implicates a rather disconcerting promise: If you play the market right, you can get rich off the scarcity of the only thing that all life on earth needs to exist.

When the Global Water Corporation took power, as one would expect, they broke every promised made. Just like politicians that campaign in poetry and govern in prose, and just like every single treaty made with the indigenous peoples of the Americas were all broken. To be fair, they did provide clean water but it was a grossly insufficient ration amount. But desperation makes men combustible like dry wood, so unknowingly to the public, it was tainted with Gamma-hydroxybutyrate (GHB) more widely known as the date-rape drug. GHB is a clear, odorless liquid that looks like water and can be added to a beverage without the person knowing it. Global Water relied on it for its sedative effects to minimize resistance to its policies and manufacture consent among the masses.

People were therefore, forced to face the smack of hard facts. There was no water justice. Accept the government's insufficient subsistence rations that required biometrics to be fed to the automated identification system or clandestinely collect illusive rainwater which constituted a contraband and risk long stretches in Nineveh's deplorable dungeons or rely on Global Water's tankers selling "safe" drinking water at exorbitant prices. The State's justification for some of these restrictions was the belief that rain harvesting would further disrupt earth's hydrological cycle with rain's natural flow back into streams and bodies of water. More accurately however, was the fact that most of the rainwater on Earth was unsafe to drink due to forever chemicals. PFAS, Per and poly-fluoroalkyl substances, that are human made, unnatural chemicals that don't break down in the environment. The Resister's rebuttal was that those streams and bodies of water were already polluted and unsafe and the bodies of water that were safe were owned by the state and access was prohibited. As for the forever chemicals present in rainwater, it was universally believed that the few that long benefited economically by the industries that produced and used these toxic chemicals, while polluting the drinking water for millions of others was not concerned about their health then and are not concerned about their health now. Especially since it was a problem they created. As a result, water became an expensive luxury and Rainwater quickly became the most valuable contraband replacing drugs, weapons and human trafficking as the most prized items on the Black Market.

Disruption became a business model. Farmers who lost their land, city dwellers that lost their middle class jobs joined the Security Forces to get a regular wage and larger water rations by enforcing the heinous codes of the new iniquitous authoritarianism. In an unjust society the only place for a just man is in prison became the mantra of the day. On the Transparency International's corruption index, Nineveh was ranked number one.

Due to the post oil depletion there are massive amounts of abandoned cars with more bikes and personal electric vehicles on the street. Other byproducts are rooftop gardens, greenhouse markets, makeshift biofuel factories and solar panel stations charging generators for last mile power delivery. Buildings were left to burn by cynical fire departments that charged exorbitant prices for its polluted fracking water waste supply for its services unless it was a Global Water property. Another dystopian byproduct was deforestation from massive wood burning resulting in a treeless city and the root cause of most of the fires.

In the nightshade of death, what does one do with all the bodies? To address this aspect of the crisis and mediate the mass graves from a drastically reduced life expectancy and exploding murder rate, necessity produced a flash of ingenuity and a glimmer of light from a humane approach that somehow always seems to survive. Nineveh became a "Death Positive" city state. Roses have thorns. Cactuses have flowers.

The paradoxical term Death Positive refers to the poetic expression Capsula Mundi. Instead of burning bodies in mass graves, a design was devised to create biodegradable pod-shaped capsules. As the body placed inside the capsule decomposes, it turns into materials that nourish new life: a tree or a garden. Those recomposed bodies would then produce a few wheelbarrows worth of a new type of Soylent Green garden soil. This program was the only source of greenery or fresh fruits and vegetables for most of the people in Nineveh and for some who could spare the water. It spurred a limited tree replanting campaign along with the indigenous bee keepers that sought to keep the species alive and assist with further fertilization needs.

CHAPTER 2
THE RESISTANCE

The city of Nineveh is ruled ruthlessly by Nimrod who has succeeded in commodifying every living resource as owner of the Global Water corporation. The depletion of the world's oil supply forced the complex use of hydrogen fuel cells, solar and wind energy, so the profiteers who shaped history had to find new things to own and control. Although water is the most common stuff on earth, only 2.5% of it is fresh, the rest is salt. And out of the freshwater, two thirds of that is locked up in glaciers and permanent snow cover, untold amounts of which have now melted into the oceans flooding the coastal cities around the world.

Before the crisis, the average person in the Western hemisphere used more than 500 liters of water daily whether by use of a toilet, shower, faucet, washing machine, leaks, bath, dishwasher, or simply wasted in half drunk plastic bottles. The human body requires less than 4 liters of water for daily consumption. The free government ration in Nineveh is only 3 liters per person per day.

The Natural Resource Defense Council has long submitted to the pressure of multinational corporations who advocate for the complete commodification and mass transport of water, the largest of them being Global Water. The biggest crisis of them all was created under the false belief that such a system was the only way to distribute water to quench the world's thirst. With billions of people worldwide in need of clean water, this enabled them to control water, food, medicine and in effect, even human beings themselves.

Virtually everything that people can buy takes water to make. The legacy of privatization enabled this takeover and created an unequal system of corporate owned property with nothing belonging to the people but their misery. In an effort to minimize protest or resistance, Nimrod created the GHB drug that pacified the masses and made them more willing to accept their fate by introducing it into the limited open market supply. Anyone drinking their 3 liter ration of secretly tainted water is a pawn of the global state. This knowledge, albeit in the hands of a few, greatly increased the value of rainwater. Obtaining it in large enough quantity to awaken the minds of the masses is the key objective of the Resistance. Only the wealthy ruling class could possibly afford access to untainted water. Unpolluted lakes, rivers and aquifers were heavily guarded leaving only rainwater, the new preeminent contraband, to be illegally harvested by the few Resisters who dare to defy the system.

After her brief encounter with the fat man with shards of glass in his ass, Evolon now enters a building where the Resisters are meeting. The door is guarded by the secret code of Yemoja Awo (translation: Mother of Fish becomes the cloud that produces rain.) After Evolon reaches the door to give the code, she passes beneath a sign quoting the great Frederick Douglass. "Without culture there can be no growth; without exertion, no acquisition; without friction, no polish; without labor, no knowledge; without action, no progress and without conflict, no victory." As her raised eyes finish reading the sign, her favorite selection from her father's collected quotes, her lowered eyes now observe a small disturbance. An older wombman is sitting behind a table near the door smoking a peace pipe, and has politely refused the entrance of a young mother with a child due to the implanted RFID chips that are now inserted into all newborns. They act as tracking devices and identification. She is turned away with 9 liters of untainted water and some food in a cart as a love offering.

Upon seeing this, Evolon slows her pace. Her eyes lock with the young mother's as she passes. She has a flashback to her childhood. She is now a thirteen year old assisting her mother Assata, who looks identical to her now adult daughter, and operates Cenotes, a free health clinic where she also provides subversive midwife services to expectant mothers of the Resistance to avoid the newborns being implanted with the RFID chips. During a delivery, the security forces invade her sanctuary in the free clinic.

"Evolon, my flower, get me some more water from the reserve tanks please." Assata instructs her daughter with force and love. The child quickly obeys her beloved mother. She retrieves the water in the back of the clinic, from a large container with a hand pump in an old fashioned clawfoot bathtub. Before she can return, Security Forces invade the room. The clinic's dead bodyguard's corpse crashes through the door and onto the floor. The new mother, still in stirrups, screams, but not from labor pains. Assata remains calm, looks up for just a moment, slows her movements, but never turns around and never stops. She continues to pull the newborn out of its mother's womb. She meticulously washes the blood from the baby's body and cuts the umbilical cord before placing the baby upon its mother's breast. She proceeds with the final stage of the delivery by removing the placenta. She is approached from behind.

A Security Force leader reads a statement. "Assata Ntu, you are hereby under arrest for violation of code 6 Section 6F of the Global State Statue; Assisted births in non-government regulated facilities."

Assata responds with her back still turned. "Please, just let this mother and child go home and I will gladly go with you" she retrieves the baby from the mother and begins to wrap the newborn in a blanket.

"The mother will be moved to a prison infirmary and this child will become a ward of the Global State in accordance with government regulations." the Security Force leader barks at her.

Assata looks deeply into the baby's eyes, smiles and then kisses it while allowing the infant to grip her pinky finger. "A global society doesn't require a global state" she announces.

During this exchange young Evolon watches from behind a curtain, holding the pan of water trembling. Her eyes are fixated on her mother's eyes. They are now locked. She sees her slip a live grenade into the warm fuzzy blanket as she slowly wraps the newborn. They share a tearful exchange as they say goodbye silently and she watches her pull the pin with her mouth.

Assata finally turns to face her would-be captors with the child extended in her arms. Young Evolon drops the pan of water which in turns spills onto the floor running across Assata's bare feet. The Security Forces's realize what is happening when Assata spits on them revealing the pin still held in her mouth between her beautiful teeth, but it is too late. "Hope for the best. Prepare for the worst" are the last words her daughter ever hears from her mother.

Upon seeing this, young Evolon runs to the back, removes the lid and then dives into the reserve water tank which is a vintage cast iron bathtub insulating her from the explosion that kills everyone else in the room. When she comes up for breath out of the water, her mental flashback ends and she returns to the entrance of the Resisters meeting where her father, Ndeble is speaking.

A small gathering of a few dozen people in the basement of an abandoned manufacturing plant are listening to a captivating speaker. Traditionally, water bearers have been women. Therefore, several women are pouring libation into the awaiting empty cups to distribute water throughout the audience.

Since New York, London and at least 33 other world cities became Atlantis, Ndeble has been the renowned leader of the Resistance. When he speaks, he ties a string of continuities between different time periods, histories, philosophies, religions and teachings. He is a revered lightworker, an elder, a sage, a guru figure who is highly respected and well read. Before he begins to speak a little girl, who is prompted by her parents, approaches him under the watchful eyes of guards. She brings a precious flower, an extremely heartfelt and costly gift in a city-state under siege by extreme water deprivation. Ndeble smiles graciously, accepts the invaluable gift. He looks into the child's eyes and lowers himself onto bended knee to thank her properly, on her level. Since all water bearers have typically been women, this gesture, combined with her youth, gives him hope for the future.

Likewise, flowers have often been a symbol of sorrow, beauty or pleasure. The term Flower Power had even once been an anti-war battle cry. But in the new context of survival in Nineveh, flowers have come to personify the sudden transition from life to death and the fragility of the human experience itself. Ndeble rises with that precious floret still in his hand and never releases his grip of it during his entire speech. The little girl watches him hold her flower with admiration and pride. When his blistering words are voiced, one feels as if one were in the presence of the living god and history being witnessed. His speech is punctuated with enthusiastic applause that comes from a deep source of passion with the fragrance of attraction that often accompanies false prophets, and not the musty funk of desperation and truth that often repels others from following poor righteous teachers:

"When in the course of human development, existing institutions prove inadequate to the needs of man, when they serve merely to enslave, rob and oppress humanity; the people have the eternal right to rebel against, and overthrow, these institutions. To be governed is to be at every operation, at every transaction, noted, register, enrolled, taxed, stamped, measured, numbered, assessed, licensed, authorized, admonished, forbidden reformed, corrected and punished! This long night of evil, injustice and social savagery which surrounds Nineveh and suppresses our people must be be brought to bear. We must bring right and justice where there is wrong and injustice. Nimrod Can't give us free speech and he can't take it away. We are born with it, like our eyes, like our ears, like our right to have access to clean drinking water in a quantity and quality sufficient for our own basic needs. This is our human right! Freedom is measured by the amount of control you have over the things upon which you are dependent. Freedom is something you assume, and then you wait for someone to try to take it away. The degree to which you resist is the degree to which you are free."

Ndeble kisses the flower and smiles at the little gift giver who returns his smile with admiration reserved only for those larger than life. Standing ovation with the small crowd chanting "Water Justice! Water Justice!"

"The drum is the centerpiece that connects the spiritual world and the physical world. It is indeed our most precious translation assistance. It allows the voices of our ancestors to speak. Let the drummers talk and I hope you will listen" Ndeble leaves the podium and the drummers take the floor while untainted water rations continue to be distributed to the audience in an orderly fashion.

Evolon moves toward the back of the room during the speech. Before she can make eye contact with Ndeble to follow him and his bodyguard to a private room, she must first pass by the bike purifiers. The men, women and children who ensure that the rainwater the resisters collect is as safe as possible to drink and free of forever chemicals. Before the polar ice caps melted flooding the coastal cities of the world behind the seas, polyfluoroalkyl substances otherwise known as PFAS, were human-made chemicals used in numerous 1st world products. Those chemicals ultimately spread into the atmosphere including the rainwater. They are called forever chemicals because they can last for thousands of years, leading to adverse health conditions that have been further weaponized by the Global Water Corporation. The Resisters circumvented the system by employing bike purifiers who provide untainted water for themselves and the struggle by using sweat equity to power a pump. Water is forced through a primary filter before moving on to an activated carbon filter and passing through a micro-filtration membrane filter. Raw water is replenished in the riders' communal tanks and reusable containers are filled at the end of the line. Evolon refills her container at the end of the line before catching up to her father.

The guard opens the door, inspects the room before they enter and leaves. We see the words "Meri-Baal" on the desk (translation: Lord of the Rebellion) sitting underneath an acrylic painting of a headshot of the CIA assassinated Prime Minister of the Congo, Patrice Lumumba.

Once alone inside the room, they embrace each other briefly with a lingering tension of love, pain, regret, shame and anger that seem to make the brief hug last a lot longer. He offers her a seat and pours them both a demitasse of water from a small pitcher before taking his seat. She throws the water back like a shot. He drinks his slowly like it was hot tea.

"For as long as I can remember, you have always drank your water in a tea cup. Why not just use a container?" Evolon asks.

"When you left my house, you were fully fed and clothed with a head as hard as petrified wood. Somehow your head is still strong but at the center of everything, telling the story of what happened, is your bottomless soul. That's because you carry around with you a 40 liter albatross that will never be filled. And even if you did fill it, you wouldn't be able to carry it. The bigger the head, the bigger the headache, the bigger the pill. But if you had a tea cup, you would be able to fill that and carry it." Ndbele explains.

"I deserve more than a tea cup and I thought weight lifting was good exercise." Evolon fires back.

"Heavy lifting can also cause spinal injuries,

herniated discs and can even tear a heart artery, which could result in death" Ndbele explains to his headstrong daughter.

"If a man, or a woman, doesn't find something they are willing to die for, then they are no longer fit to live" she flatly retorts.

Ndbele impatiently inhales and exhales while drumming his fingers on his desk with simultaneous pride and frustration before he finally speaks. "Influence is a science. Passion is only a fruit, I am afraid. So my dear woman child, did you find Saisir?"

She shoots back, after perceiving to be chastised, "If I had found him you would have heard he was dead already."

His drumming fingers become a clenched fist and he hits the desk in an outburst of fatherly discipline. "Damn it Evolon! Come back to the world! Your head is harder than the ancient Olmec statues! Can't you see past your own hatred? Are you evolving or devolving? You must master self like you have mastered your weapons."

"I am a weapon" Evolon spits through gritted teeth like her mother's last words with a grenade pin in her mouth.

"Then master self. Taking life can protect life, but

it does not give it. We need him alive to even begin to bargain with the likes of Nimrod. We must not become that which we detest" he explains.

Evolon sucks her teeth and retorts, "Look, your steel toe angel speech out there was very nice per usual. But to what degree are you free bargaining with this thorny devil?

"When I look up and see my people before me, I feel elated. Untainted human beings are the cloth I need around me. But don't suffer from the confusion of Babel. Nimrod's reputation as a king who has sinned against god is most well deserved. But he is no more the devil than I am god. His true story is actually one of how a nation conquered the world and failed its own people. He is simply another man corrupted by power. The blood of his only son is worthless to us" he replies.

Evolon snaps back, 'Would the blood of your own daughter be more valuable?"

Ndeble lowers his head to conceal emotion, "Much more valuable than my own, yes." He takes a deep breath and declares with blistering intent in his eyes, raising his head high "But I would sacrifice both to alleviate the suffering of the people of Nineveh. We have only three days of water left if it doesn't rain, and you are the only one who can get close enough to Saisir. Without you and your unique abilities of weapon mastery, Nimrod's plan to dry us out will destroy the Resistance."

In a much softer and reflective tone Evolon inhales and responds "I would give a pint of blood for a long hot bath in the finest artesian water right now."

"I am afraid that we do to have enough blood for that luxury right now. I, too, dream of the day I can take a long hot shower whenever I want for as long as I want. I have limited myself to bathing in the rain since you were a little girl. Now all I have is a river of words in which to bathe, but every movement requires sacrifice." he says.

Evolon eyes a framed quote on her father's desk she hasn't noticed before. She picks it up and reads it out loud.

"I always like walking in the rain, so no one can see me crying."
                                                    –Charlie Chaplin

Her naturally sarcastic tone returns immediately after putting the frame down, "God has certainly taken care of us."

"Do you know the kangaroo rat can go its entire life without ever drinking a single drop of water? They survive primarily on the seeds and beans high in water content" Ndeble shares.

"And the power of their jump can also effectively defend against rattlesnake bites" Evolon replies.

Ndbele visibly concedes this point. "When you put wildflower honey in your bush tea, do you ever pay homage to the bee? I too share your contempt for the hopes of a benevolent god, but just because you have a nightmare doesn't mean you stop dreaming. It is true, terrible things have happened on god's watch and it is a piece of cowardice to fully submit to the will of god if it impedes action. Faith without work is truly dead. Which is why I never bring god talk into my business." Ndbele confesses.

"In every waking moment of my life for as long as I can remember, I have always felt the absence of god." Evolon confesses.

Ndeble takes another long slow sip of water from his tea cup. He sits it down delicately before he speaks, "The sun rises on the evil and on the good. Just like rain falls on the just and the unjust alike. The coexistence of good and evil is like a field of wheat and weeds. In gathering the weeds you might pull up some of the wheat along with them. So you let the wheat and the weeds grow together until the harvest. And that time is now upon us."

Evolon's eyes catch fire and she speaks through gritted teeth again, "I have my sickle sharpened and ready. I've been patient but, where I'm concerned, patience has its limits. Take it too far, and it's cowardice."

The great martial artist Bruce Lee once said "Be like water making its way through cracks. Do not be assertive, but adjust to the object, and you shall find a way around or through it. If nothing with you stays rigid, outward things will disclose themselves. Empty your mind, be formless. Shapeless, like water. If you put water into a bottle it becomes the bottle. You put it in a teapot, it becomes the teapot. Now, water can flow or it can crash. Be water, my child." Ndeble cautions her.

Their meeting is interrupted when Bethlehem, a new part of Ndbele's security team, enters the room with the presence of a warrior to whisper into Ndbele's ear. He is a bold but quiet man of great strength that has been specifically entrusted by Ndbele himself with a secret mission unbeknownst to anyone else, including Evolon or even Bethlehem himself. Ndbele reaches for a pen and paper and speaks as he begins to write. "We have just learned the possible location of one of Saisir's concubines. You go there and wait for him. I hope his reputation is well deserved." He hands her the paper. "Bethlehem you go with her and make sure she doesn't kill anyone unnecessarily" he adds.

Evolon is shocked. "I work alone."

Ndeble finally finishes his tea cup of water. "A bowhead whale had a forehead so powerful that they could break up to two feet of ice sheets just to breathe. They conquered some of the harshest conditions in the world. But they only existed in the Arctic seas. When the polar caps melted and the arctic was destroyed, they too became extinct. We all are here due to a delicate balance of chance and circumstance. When the Amazon was still the lungs of the planet, transatlantic dust from the Sahara Desert fertilized its rainforest with phosphorous. No one makes it on their own. So never, ever make the mistake of thinking you are alone" in a matter of fact toned response.

Evolon feels the warmth of his statement and receives it. "What if he doesn't show in time?"

Ndeble pours the last of the water left in the pitcher into his tea cup and watches as the last drop slowly falls. He then raises the cup and puts it to his lips, still sipping it slowly like it was hot tea. "We need the patience to wait for the mud to settle in the water and the water to become clear. Until then, let's all pray it rains soon. Death is our deadline."

Evolon and Bethlehem exit the room leaving Ndeble to his reading. He opens the book Seven Pillars of Wisdom: A Triumph by T.E. Lawrence and begins to underline his favorite passage.

All men dream: but not equally. Those who dream by night in the dusty recess of their minds wake up in the day to find it was vanity, but the dreamers of the day are dangerous men, for they may act upon their dreams with open eyes, to make it possible.

CHAPTER 3

SEX IN THE CITY

Evolon and Bethlehem traveled to their destination on her motorcycle. Driving in Nineveh is in itself a most dangerous and precarious undertaking. Large sinkholes that resulted from depleted groundwater are scattered around the entire metropolis and throughout the countryside. With abandoned cars everywhere, and several sinkholes scattered on the roadways, one must be a very attentive driver. Not to mention the robbers who occasionally set up makeshift roadblocks to pounce on weaker prey.

The spokes of the speeding front wheel contrast with the passing electrified fencing that guards the largest reservoir in Nineveh. It is highly fortified. Children are often seen throwing metal objects at the fence to watch in amazement when the sparks fly, like they are playing with fireworks. This is a favorite pastime for younger children. Older kids prefer to take their slingshots and try to shoot down the drones, making them neighborhood heroes whenever they are successful. Here, Evolon is the determined and focused driver while Bethlehem's legs wrap around her. His hands squeeze the rear handle as the joyous but valiant rider leans deftly into every curve. They move like expert hand dancers whose souls are in sync with each other. The brief sun sets into the horizon with its remaining light reflecting off the surface of the water onto the faces of their black helmets. Evolon's masculine energy usually makes most men feel feminine, but she begins to sense it doesn't intimidate the robust Bethlehem at all, which in turn makes her actually feel more feminine. But her resolve forces a more resilient determination to be even less receptive.

It has gotten dark and more dangerous. Since inadequate access to clean water, nutritious food and poverty are the leading causes of violence, we see the worst that poverty and desperation have to offer. Food stores are guarded like banks in the old world order. Some even have snipers on the roof to dispel would be looters. Water trucks have armored vehicle protections. Walking down a street on the Southside of Nineveh eating or drinking would be the equivalent of counting a large amount of cash alone on the most dangerous street in the largest cities, during a blackout that lasts forever. Composed of nows where the lights never come back on. Creating a long dangerous night where the sun never rises on a glorious morning.

The question of whether poverty is a cause of violence is a question for a sociologist, but the question of whether violence is the cause of poverty is a philosopher's question. But Victor Hugo said, " If the soul is left in darkness, sins will be committed. The guilty one is not he who commits the sin, but the one who causes the darkness." Unfathomable sins had been committed against the people of Nineveh, and unlike wealth, only misery trickles down. Whereas fascism throws rocks and hides its hands. So he without sin, be the first to cast the stone.

Upon arrival they dismount and secure the bike out of sight from the street into relative safety. As they approach the building's location they both simultaneously pause momentarily to observe a beautiful brightly colored mural on the wall next to the building that has somehow escaped the ruins that have ravaged Nineveh for generations. The words "the next great liberation movement will come from the same place the last one came from, from below" are graffiti styled high art in fire engine red, jungle green and as black as indigofera tinctoria. Along with these iconoclastic words appeared an alchemical sign for the element of water, a triangle balancing a circle on its point.

"Symbols are door ways to myth and info." Bethlehem reflects to himself.

"There is no revolution without art" Evolon responds accordingly.

During their following mutually silent pause to enjoy a moment of artistic rebellious beauty, a black cat crosses their path directly overly one mural and adverting their eyes to yet another mural. With the words, "Darkness is a special space. You can see things in the dark. Stevie Wonder, Ray Charles, Helen Keller all saw something special in the dark. Find a dark spot and learn something." Nineveh is a dark city filled with feral cats indifferent to human contact and more adept to rodent management, but this particular black cat undifferentiated by chaos stroked its body around Evolon's left leg. In the Old World, dogs were often the more popular pet. But in the New World they come to realize that when dogs lap water up, they spill water all around whereas cats are neater and more efficient drinkers as they touch only the surface of the water. This is why the real purpose of the proliferation of cats in Nineveh is that most animals have an extraordinary sense of smell which helps them determine whether to drink or abandon the idea of drinking from any particular water source and cats were clearly more water efficient. Since the outbreak of Cyanobacteria, feral cats have been invaluable resources to ensure safe water quality. In fact, Bedouins had been known to follow bats to locate hard to find water sources.

As Bethlehem squats to pet their feline friend, they are approached by a well stocked street hustler in a non-threatening manner. "Peace, if you prepared to fight for it! I got switchblades, tasers, stun guns, brass knuckles, billy clubs, pepper spray, mace, handcuffs, razor blades, concealed purses and wallets baby. I even got the aluminum adhesive patches to block RFID chips. What you need?" he offers his pitch while displaying his wares.

His offer is gently refused and Evolon hands him a tangor fruit from her coat, a most generous offering. Even Bethlehem is pleasantly surprised to see her exhibit such generosity and compassion. "What else do you have in your 40 liter bucket?" He asks.

She is surprised at his knowledge of this information and realizes that her private conversation with her father may not have been private and now views him with a bit of suspicion when she mentally questions and recalls him whispering in her father's ear in her presence in the first place. "It ain't no goddamn tea cup, you can bet that." She snaps back with low grade feelings of betrayal.

They finally survey the building looking for the best access point for them to reach the penthouse suite. The lobby isn't heavily guarded but they didn't want to spook their target, so they decided to scale the narrow balconies up to the 13th floor. Once they got to the luxury studio apartment they found Saisir's concubine Asherah, voluptuous and beautiful in the bathroom surrounded by her humble savage soy candle lights burning around the large step-down bath tub the size of a jacuzzi, having a luxurious bubble bath, eating seeded grapes while drinking a chilled bottle of Global Water's finest artesian water.

Evolon briefly envies the vibe that Asherah has created. Even more briefly, she enjoys the fragrance of the humble savage candles that unbeknownst to her, Asherah makes herself with Saisir being her biggest and most enthusiastic client. Then she grabs her by the hair, snatching it all the way back with envy and righteous indignation covering her mouth. Bethlehem grabs her wet nude body wrapping it with large towels while lifting her out of the tub but treating her as respectfully as possible. They handcuff her to the bed and duct tape her mouth wet and confused. Then they sit and wait like patient fishermen enjoying the beautiful humble savage smells while the candles burn and just like all soldiers who shamelessly enjoy the spoils of war, they raid the kitchen to see what they could find.

Several hours later Saisir, a pretty boy with a small and fragile build uncommon for the normal obesity of the elite class, arrives with his own key. He calls out to his lover who allegedly has romantic music still playing for him. He first makes his way to the restroom. As he relieves himself, he notices the bathtub is still full. He calls out to Asherah. "Babe, I told you. You don't have to conserve your water with me. I got you." There is no response. He flushes the toilet and pulls the plug in the bathtub. He helps himself to one of the seeded grapes. He then ventures into the bedroom where he finds her tied up. He smiles. "Oh, we're playing that game tonight are we? But tell me, how did you manage to tie yourself up?" he asks with his hands on his hips still puzzled and swallows the seeded grape whole.

Evolon steps out the shadows of the corner of the room "She didn't."

"Who the fuck are you!" Saisir screams and gags on the grape choking.

"The truth, and we came to get down" Bethlehem replies.

Before Bethlehem and Evolon are able to fully subdue him, Saisir's initial gagging scream was still loud enough that it was able to alert his security who immediately invade the room and they engage in hand to hand combat. Evolon decisively dominates both men simultaneously until Bethlehem, after securing Saisir, prevents her from killing one of them by capturing her hand wielding a large knife held to the bulging vein inches from the moribund man's neck.

"The first thought is the spirit. The second is the mind. This is not a neural interactive simulation. Just a man doing his job to survive." He whispers to her while she continues to test his strength as her arm trembles.

Evolon eventually relaxes her grip, calms herself, stands up and puts her balisong, a butterfly switchblade, away in grand fashion. "Well then on second thought, I'm going to take a bath. You sit here and baby sit."

Evolon shamelessly begins to undress with her clothes falling to the floor on her way to the bath. She has stripped down topless to her underwear by the time she reaches the bathroom door revealing a beautifully exotic Wabori, which is a Japanese style tattoo commonly called irezumi that literally means inserting ink. Her artwork covers her back from the top of her left shoulder to the bottom of her right hip. It depicts a large wildfire in a forrest above a much smaller cascading waterfall descending slowly over rocks into a stream with vivid colors of red and blue for the immense fire and the miniscule body of water, thereby visualizing the dramatic summary for the task at hand of their life's work.

She shamelessly picks up Asherah's unfinished bottle of Global Water's upscale untainted artesian water and gulps it down while being watched closely by both Bethlehem and Saisir until she picks up the remaining seeded grapes before closing the door topless with her back to them. Bethlehem then smacks Siasir on the back of his head when he realizes he was also enjoying the view too watching her undress just as mesmerized. Bethlehem secures the security, calls for transport and afterwards, the victorious duo leaves with Saisir. Asherah is left handcuffed and unharmed to the bed still wrapped in a large towel with the bodies of Saisir's security drugged, gagged and bounded on the floor bruised, but still alive.

While in the car, the State radio broadcasts commercial plays with a weather forecast calling for no rain in sight to the majority of the occupants frustrations, immediately followed by a commercial for Global Water: "From the glaciers of the arctic to the Blue Nile of the Sudan; we bring you what the world thirsts for.... Global Water."

Now Saisir sits in a large room somewhere in a Southside Nineveh basement surrounded by darkness tied to a chair with a hood over his head sitting beneath a low hanging light. The hood is then snatched off his head and the duct tape from his mouth is removed painfully along with a few hairs from his light facial hair. The interrogation now begins. As his eyes are as wide open as a snake and racing inside his head squinting fast, struggling to adjust to the low light in the darkness of the room.

"What, are you crazy?" Saisir screams.

"In a world of insanity, it is the strong that goes crazy. It is the weak that pretends that there is nothing wrong." Ndbele said with his back to him pouring himself a teacup of water.

"Do you people know who I am?" he exclaims.

Evolon leans her face into the light for him to see and uses her index finger to push his forehead far back "Of course we know who you are. That's why you're here."

"Then you must know my father will kill your entire families!" he barks at her spitefully.

Ndeble steps into the light and throws the rest of the precious untainted water in his cup into Saisir's face in a defiant libation and rare glimpse of rage looking him directly in the eyes inches between them staring face to face before circling behind him to continue "Your father of lies has already killed our families! We are here because they aren't. And you are going to help us save the rest."

Saisir blinks fast, shakes his head and then laughter booms wholeheartedly from his wet face "Oh yeah? And why would I do that?" His eyes mockingly follow Ndeble and Evolon circling around him like sharks.

Evolon racks a single barrel pistol gripped shotgun, but with the safety still on, in the dark and puts the barrel to his nose "Because I'll stick a shotgun up your ass and leave you here for the rats."

Her words to the wise were sufficient. This brings an abrupt ending to Saisir's disingenuous laughter as he now swallows with difficulty and begins to sweat "Oh. I mean, how would I do that?"

Ndeble puts his hand on his shoulder and leans into Saisir's ear "You are going to supply us with three truck loads of untainted water every thirteen days to let the world know we have gone as far as we can accepting drops from the faucet."

"I thought you people were water boosters. What you tired of drinking rainwater?" he asks.

Evolon steps back into the light with the shotgun thrown over her shoulder "We capture a half litre of water per square meter for every centimeter of rainfall. In order to provide an adequate amount of untainted water for all of our people we would need a catchment area the size of a fucking coliseum!"

"Look if you have a problem with the current water market distribution model take it up with the Natural Resource Defense Council. This has nothing to do with me!" Saisir pleads his case.

"A reasonable man adjusts to his environment. An unreasonable man does not. All progress, therefore, depends on the unreasonable man. Rebellion is our only grievance system. We represent the Village Resistance Council and we are not here in need of retaining a public interest lawyer" Ndeble offers the rebuttal.

Evolon interjects "And if you are not going to help us, we are not in need of you!" She puts the loaded shotgun to the side of his face again, but this time she takes the safety off and Saisir see's her do it as well as that of her father and Bethlehem who flinches to intercede on Ndbele's command that he never receives.

Saisir, oblivious to their silent interaction, now sees a rat almost big as a cat run past the door and begins to drip with more sweat "Damn welcome to Global Water, may I help you please?

"Three truck loads of 200 litre drums every thirteen days!" Ndeble repeats himself.

"That's impossible!" Saisir declares.

"Impossible is just a big word thrown around by small men who find it easier to live in the world they've been given than to explore the power that have to change it. Impossible is not a fact. It's an opinion. Impossible is not a declaration. It's a dare. Impossible is potential. Impossible is temporary. Impossible is nothing." Ndbele's volume increases with each word and ends with him speaking through gritted teeth.

"Muhammad Ali, the greatest warrior poet" Bethlehem interrupts.

"What are you? A Guru or Sultan?" Saisir asks in honest disbelief to Ndbele's incredulous statement.

"We shall see if this is tantric yoga or religion. But I have found that religion is often so heavenly bound that it is of no earthly good to me. Faith without works is indeed dead. Which is why the church is a hiding place. Before being burned alive by the Spaniards, chief Hatuey of the island of Hispaniola was asked if he wanted to accept Christianity and get to Heaven. Hatuey asked if Spaniards go to Heaven, to which the priest said they do. Hatuey then stated that he'd rather go to hell where he wouldn't see such cruel people. Therefore, we refuse to wait for the promise of getting to heaven. We would rather choose to make a difference here and now. So we don't pray for water. We use our bodies and minds to take it, in 200 litre drums" Ndbele states emphatically.

Saisir shakes his head "Now how long do you expect me to do that?"

Evolon screams in his face "Forever! As long as you continue to use the suffering women of Nineveh as your personal sex slaves or the next time you put your little dick in some pussy it might have razor blades in it!"

Saisir again swallows nervously, taps his feet on the floor and this time squeezes his narrow legs together to comfort his threatened family jewels in an effort to compose himself "Hey, calm down! I'm just saying that it would be impossible' he pauses to correct himself. 'I mean it would be very difficult to obtain that much untainted water on a regular basis without detection. The government supply is metered, rationed and heavily guarded. You know that."

"How much would it cost for you to call your grandmother a bitch to her face?" Evolon asks.

Saisir is astonished.

Ndeble puts his ever present tea cup he has leisurely refilled during the interrogation to his lips again sipping slowly and still circling Saisir like a relentless shark "All of us owe something to somebody else. We didn't get here by ourselves. The price of liberty is less than the cost of repression. So, the difficult we do immediately. The impossible, well it just takes a little longer. It is our overstanding that your father is quite fond of beautifully dying flowers Saisir and has a personal greenhouse with a dedicated private water supply."

Saisir is visibly surprised that they are aware of this information and finally realizes that the Resistance is far more formidable than the common water boosters he originally mistook them for "Yeah, that's right. He would rather be a warrior in the garden, than a gardener at war" he boasts boldly in a perfidious display of tough solidarity with his father.

Ndeble continues to slowly sip his water from his tea cup while walking circles around him, pacing the room and reads the transition of his thinking by Saisir's body language correctly and briefly offers the glimpse of a rare smile on his face when he finally comes to a stand still with his face starring in his cup "When I was a child, I prayed to god for a bike. It never came. So when I came of age, I stole one and my prayers were answered." He looks directly into Saisir's eyes of stupefaction. "Well you're going to switch our water with his. The Flower of Life is sacred geometry. We empty your trucks and then we fill them."

An emotionally defeated Saisir responds with more perplexity "But what will that do to the flowers?

"What the fuck do you think it does to us? We touched you before. We can touch you again. Remember that, pretty boy." Evolon has the last word as Bethlehem puts the black hood back over his head.

Saisir is returned to his concubine relatively unharmed and arouses his guards who are, to a lesser extent, relatively unharmed. He pays them extra for their pain, suffering and most importantly, their continued silence and sends them home. He finds his beautiful lover Asherah still tied to the bed asleep with her humble savage candles still burning. He removes the handcuffs and duct tape as gently as he possibly can awakening her. She throws her arms and chapped wrists around him "Saisir! You're alive! Oooh baby, I thought you were dead for sure! Who were those people, terrorists?"

Saisir begins to lotion her wrists and massage them. "No, just some people I owe from a gambling debt trying to scare me. I am so sorry about all this. I gave them what they wanted after I kicked their asses for doing this to you and now everything is fine. They won't be coming back here" he promises her.

"You are so brave baby" Asherah says seductively. She hugs him sweetly, kisses him softly and wraps her legs around him. Her towel falls off her beautiful body while she slowly undresses him and they begin to engage in passionate lovemaking.

Saisir abruptly stops the foreplay and gently grabs her by her sore wrists looking deeply and directly into her eyes as if he was desperately searching for her soul for an answer while tenderly continuing to massage the marks on her wrists "You don't have any razor blades in the house do you?"

Asherah looks at him incredulously "What?"

CHAPTER 4

WATER IS LIFE

In the car on the way back to the resistance stronghold Evolon and Ndeble sit in the backseat with both looking out the window of the opposite sides of the car reflecting on the past interrogation. Ndeble is a skilled chess player thinking several moves ahead and deliberating the next moves of the middle game whereas Evolon is still preoccupied with the moves already made in the opening game. He sees chess as the three dimensional game it is of time, space and ideas. Whereas, his daughter only sees the war game as a black and white board in front of her with us vs them. Bethlehem is driving and his eyes and Evolon's eyes catch each other briefly in the rearview mirror which reminds her of her unfounded apprehension of Bethlehem's presence before she speaks impatiently while addressing her father. "I don't know why you didn't ask for more water. We could have gotten a larger shipment if we demanded a ransom. This arrangement isn't going to last for long. There's no guarantee he is even going to honor our demands" she blurts out while still looking out the window.

In turn, her father responds slowly while still looking out the opposite window as well. "First of all, you never take more than you can carry Miss 40 litre bucket. The greatest empires have all fallen because of waste, abuse, greed and most importantly, over confidence. Unrestrained power always leads to abuse. Second of all, Saisir is controlled by fear and his vices. We threatened to remove the only comfort he has in this life. He will abide. Thus we have achieved two very important counter intelligence objectives. First we are able to track the supply trucks back to the source and secondly the more deliveries that are made the higher the chance of Nimrod finding out" he explains.

Evolon turns to her father suddenly. Her eyes do not seem to accept the truths that her untrained ears just heard. "You mean you actually want Nimrod to find out?"

"Then he will turn on his son and we will take the stage and step in to try save him, if we can, thereby making him a lifelong ally if we are successful. If we fail, we would have been able to capture thousands of liters of untainted water to multiply our numbers by the hundreds like the petals of a flower that follows the Fibonacci sequence while simultaneously dividing theirs" he says matter of factly after finally turning to face his only child.

Evolon notices Bethlehem is writing in his little notebook on the steering wheel. He seems to always be writing whenever her father speaks. "Are you ambidextrous? Watch the road! There's sinkholes everywhere. Why are you always writing in your little book of numbers anyway?" she asks.

He looks at her again through the rearview mirror and responds after closing his little book of numbers and putting his hands on the steering wheel at 10 o'clock and 2 o'clock "We are all writing a book. The horrors of Nineveh can kill one's spirit. Writing keeps the mind and imagination alive. So I record history as it unfolds with guerrilla penmanship. It is always dangerous to forget the lessons of history. The diameter of your knowledge my dear is not the product of your ideas, it is the circumference of your activities. Knowledge speaks. Wisdom listens. But we must never forget that imagination is more important than knowledge. They can kill us, but they can not prevent us from altering history by recording it accurately. Until the lions have their own historians, the tales of the hunted will always continue to glorify the hunter. I am here to tell the lion's story."

The remainder of the return journey is done in silence.

So far throughout history the responses of the people to injustice from their governments have all been directly or indirectly geared toward appealing to the moral consciousness of those who have no morals or consciousness. For the first time in history the success of a struggle was largely depending on the immorality, violence and greed of the oppressor, thereby guaranteeing ultimate victory. The power of a tyrant is measured by the endurance of the people. Or as they like to say in Nineveh, the amount of shit you can take is equal to the sum total of the same amount of shit you shall receive.

Ndbele was right. Saisir honored the agreement. The arrangement process was working and untainted water deliveries were being made with the required exchanges in return. After they replenished their reserves, they resumed their subversive water distribution program moving just like flying rivers. As long as the Resistance could provide water, their support and followers would continue to grow. Breaking their mind and spirits free from the mind controlling sedative found in the rationed public supply that effectively prevented large scale uprising as a tool of social control.

Finally, the drought is broken and it rains. Whenever it rains in Nineveh it is a water riot and cause celebre no matter what time of the day. Church bells rings. A long chorus of toilets flush around the city. The streets are filled with talking drums. Everyone runs outside to be drenched and enjoy the brief liberation of the torturous stench of urine stained streets and the lack of want. No one but the elite uses umbrellas properly. On the Southside of Nineveh, all umbrellas are turned upside down for instant rainwater catchment. People are bathing outside, washing clothes, brushing their teeth, making love on rooftops, even some dancing in the rain and as expected, massive numbers of people are collectively working together to collect the maximum amount of rainwater the best way they can. Organized groups of Resisters implemented the same method used by firefighters before the advent of hand-pumped fire engines, they created a bucket brigade as human supply lines filled buckets of water captured from covert catchment areas that had not been destroyed by Security Forces for being successfully concealed and hidden. All this of course, is highly illegal and results in some arrests by the Security Forces that fruitlessly brutalize violators for this, but the shear size of the open civil disobedience are well beyond their capacity to be contained. For a time in their frustration, they even treated the weather forecasts like banned books.

The exact forecast of rain had become a kind of classified information not to be shared with the public. This only served to corrupt the weather forecasters that profited from sharing that coveted information and also made the Resistance skilled in observation and ancient knowledge of water patterns. The classic practice of wetting your index finger held up high to determine the direction of the wind was effective when applied with the knowledge that weather moves in from the west. Westerly winds indicate dry weather because they suggest the wet weather is already to the east. Just like the sun rises in the east, the Resisters knew that easterly winds suggest that rain is coming. In the end, the ineffective ban on forecasts were lifted, to the dismay of the forecasters and their short-lived lucrative racket. The Security Forces had to mostly limit their harassment to those caught transporting large containers of untainted water after the fact and not during the cause celebre of the open water rebellions themselves.

Rain puts everyone in Nineveh in a good mood with a sigh of momentarily relief. Even the melancholic disposition of Evolon is penetrated and subdued to the extent that she attends a club scene in a popular venue called "The Nile Gallery" with a poet on stage with a great trio of musicians and the audience in a brief call and response.

"Water is life... Water is life.. Water is life... Wata is life... The world is pregnant with change and her water is about to break.

I see the midwife in the mirror as the day draws nearer praying the premature baby would wait to make its entrance into the world that's war torn for so long that the peaceful child is breach born feet first prepared for the streets worse struggle and strife suffering and sacrifice until it exits a hearse feet first. What's your self worth?

If Water is life... Water is life... Water is life.. Wata is life... and you can't afford to buy it. In Nairobi babies drink coca-cola cause the water's so dirty their parent's don't want to try it. Privatized commercialized commodified water is causing global riots while ignoble pirates privatize commercialize commodify human rights stealing life selling rights choosing between daughters and wife.

Water is life.. Water is life.. Water is life... Wata is life..

Are you thirsty enough to fight? Or are your biblical eyes blinded by pagan sights in fear of patriotic might chaotic nights change is in the air forming dark clouds black angels and fire fights.

Its about to rain fags and dikes drumbeats and mics bullet or knife Water is life... Water is life... Water is life... Wata is life..."

We find Evolon sitting alone at a table drinking a French Connection watching the performance. The band takes a break and the DJ takes over with Fela Kuti's Water No Get Enemy playing as the entire enchanted crowd chants all the words and floods the dance floor. She deeply admires the movements of the crowd as they dance the dance of life, especially that of those who danced alone. Ko s'shun tole se k'o ma lo'mi o. Nothing without water. She is finally joined by an uninvited Bethlehem who doesn't drink and whispers into her ear from behind "You know that is very bad for you?" He pauses for a response before he takes a seat across from her at the small table.

Evolon looks down into her drink upon hearing his voice. She then raises her head, her eyes and her unique glass "Why it's the brother that writes but doesn't talk sitting here without a lion's pen running his mouth. Well I'll promise you Baba Jr. that this will not kill me. My drinking vessel is carved from amethyst crystals to prevent drunkenness. The drinking of cognac is to soothe the wounds of those who suffer. Especially for those fighting for the universal solvent." She puts the beautiful glass to her lips and sips it slowly like her father with water in a tea cup.

Bethlehem smiles warmly "that is good to know, those that don't make time for their wellness will make time for their illness and I do seem to recall a lot of bloodshed over alcohol during the Prohibition Period in America also that seems to reflect to a lesser extent, the dire straits we find ourselves in now fighting for the universal solvent. But I was talking about you sitting here with your back to the door."

She puts the drink down "What? Please! You could have gotten shot just walking over here." She motions over his shoulder. Bethlehem turns around to find the steely eyes of a very large burly bartender who is not smiling.

He then tips his hat to him and turns back around to find the cold eyes of the woman that warms his hard heart and says "Ahhh, my true warrior queen. A freedom fighter who will not abandon the battle field until the war is won."

"I would die before I quit. I give my hand, my heart and my head to the total struggle. I found power in my pain. It elevated me and strengthen my resolve. Now what do you want? Are you following me? I know you ain't here for the music. Your type probably don't even like art" she says accusatorially.

"Oh to the contraire my dear. Art is like water. It takes the form of whatever situation you put it in. 'There can be no revolution without art.' He smiles to pause for her reaction after repeating her own earlier words. She remembers but he receives no such acknowledgement. 'When the drums sounded our ancestors gathered their knives and listened to the wind. Great artists bring the war drums to the forefront. Normally, whatever that is, they are the backbone of society. The mighty genius of Paul Robeson said 'Artists are the gatekeepers of truth and are civilization's radical voice.' I believe art is the attempt to find meaning in a world that doesn't make sense. That's why we dance. To find meaning. Every child is an artist until someone or something beats it out of them. As for me, I am a lover of fine poetry myself" he clears his throat and takes a breath before reciting a poem:

"If we must die, let it not be like hogs hunted and penned in an inglorious spot while round us bark the mad and hungry dogs, making their mock at our accursed lot. If we must die, let us nobly die, so that our precious blood may not be shed in vain; then even the monsters we defy shall be constrained to honor us though dead: O kinsmen: We must meet the common foe: though far outnumbered let us

*show us brave, and for their thousand blows deal
one deathblow: What though before us lays the open
grave: Like men we'll face the murderous, cowardly
pack, pressed to the wall, dying, but fighting back!"*

Evolon is mildly impressed. "Wow! That was almost beautiful. You actually wrote that? she asks.

He pulls out his water bottle and smiles as he puts it to his lips.

"I am afraid not. That was 'If We Must Die' from Claude McKay. He wrote that lion's story with an iron pen and a blood diamond point over two hundred years ago. I believe poems come more from a fascination with observation than from an idea. It is the only poem I have ever committed to memory. It reminds me a lot of you" he confesses to her.

"Really? So tell me Langston, what does the busboy poet want? she asks pointedly.

"I have an important message for you" he replies.

"Oh yeah? And what news of good tidings have you been ordered to bring to me you fucking robot?" she coldly asks.

Bethlehem leans in with his answer "I am here to inform you that I will be the man that marries you."

Levity enters the space, but Evolon refuses to

laugh "Is that right?"

Bethlehem leans back in his seat "Yes, that's right and two more just like you."

Levity momentarily finds its mark. Finally, a chip in her armor is visible and Evolon is overcome by restrained laughter in the form of a dry chuckle. They mutually enjoy the pleasure the brief moment provides. Until her usual melancholic disposition returns and she begins to reflect.

"I could never marry nor have children in a place like this" she offers.

"And why not?" he inquires further.

"Even abortions don't make you forget the lost of life sucked from us. You know very well what happens to the children who are born here and to their parents. Putting a hole in the soul of another mother. They will die of terrible diseases, they will be killed or die of starvation or water deprivation and no one will mourn for them. Their lives will be like manure on the ground as their neglected bodies decompose as fertilizer in a capsule. Their blood will stain these urine stench streets never to be washed away until it rains again" she exclaims before finishing her drink and motions to the bear sized bartender for another.

Bethlehem reaches for her hand. She accepts it

as she blinks quickly to fight back a tear and holds her head down rather than face him and allow him to see it run down her face. "I hope god is not a woman" she spits through gritted, grinding teeth.

"Why is that?" He presses her hand firmly.

She looks up with eyes as dry as the mouths of the poorest people in Nineveh to face him before replying. "Because I only kill men."

"Well, I see your pain of misandry doesn't contain any political correctness. We are both at war with the world, but you cannot also be at war with yourself. Traveling is searching. Home is what has been found" he replies.

"Then I am going hunting. I am the hunter" Evolon declares.

"Zora Neale Hurston said that 'I have been in sorrows kitchen and licked out all the pots. Then I have stood on the peek mountain wrapped in rainbows, with a harp and a sword in my hands.' I think what she was trying to say is that pain is inevitable... but misery is optional. The most ugly and tragic lives birth the most beautiful and powerful music, dance, comedy, art. You must always remember that roses become compost; compost feeds the garden for the growth of new roses. Just like all those decomposing bodies in these capsules creating wheelbarrows of organic fertile garden soil. And to plant a garden is to believe in tomorrow. You are prepared to fight for liberation. But are you prepared to also fight for happiness? It sounds as if you're unafraid to die, but too scared to live" he submits.

Evolon is triggered.

"Scared? I ain't scared of nothing! I am filled with the spirit of Yaa Asantewaa! I am the black gold of the sun! My anger is an eternal fire that can consume anything!" she declares.

Bethlehem leans in again "Including you. You tear out weakness and wear your strength well. Ancestral memory is a powerful weapon. But the thing about supreme militancy is if you are not careful with the sword, you can slice yourself. You must differentiate between flowers and weeds. We must not destroy them both to get rid of the other. The source of the pain is the cause of the pain. The prescription for the cure rests with an accurate diagnosis of the cause of the disease."

"Nothing will ever change here! Meteorites have more rights than our people! " She screams through firmly gritted teeth. "They dominate us in economics, education, entertainment, labor, law, politics, religion, sex, war and health! I would rather be dead than to see us continue the way we are for another generation."

"The problem and the solution are at the root. The Black Panther Albert Woodfox survived over four decades of the most brutal solitary confinement in the largest prison system the world has ever seen. If he could survive, we can survive" Bethlehem boldly announces.

"Survival is the lowest form of existence" Evolon retorts.

"Some things must be handled with clay covered hands in order to mold the situation to our liking. We are the warrior potters as this earth spins on the potter's wheel. If we don't like what we see we must be willing to start all over again." Bethlehem said.

"Even a potter's hands need water to stay wet." Evolon responds.

"You should try therapeutic screaming sometime when you are alone. It is good for the soul. We will win Evolon. You act on a higher level. Think on a higher level. Oppressed people cannot remain oppressed forever. To believe with all our heart in our people and the righteousness and victory of our struggle. Ndbele has foreseen it. Your father is a divine prophet." Bethlehem said.

Evolon composes herself and takes a deep breath "No he's not, an organic intellectual with a gift of actualization perhaps, but not a prophet. A prophet is respected everywhere except in his hometown and by his own family. My father has no love outside the Resistance. True loyalty and respect is about standing in a principle. So when people respect you and are loyal to you, it's not that they are loyal to you. They are loyal to the principle. It's because of that principle that they would burn books that even mentioned his name."

"This is true. But there is no greater love than a man that would lay down his life for his loved ones. And I would go down to the world of the dead to follow your father and you. If I asked for a lifetime and only got a moment, it would be time will spent" he offers in an attempt to console her and seduce her.

Evolon's drink arrives. She sings softly swishing the lone ice cube in her glass, "Water, water everywhere not a drop to drink" while her eyes are lost in the motion of the swishing French Connection in her glass.

"I love your voice" Bethlehem shares.

Evolon turns her head to look away. She sees her beloved mother's smiling face. She sees all the moments she cared for her. "When I was little, my mother used to love to hear me sing. She particularly loved that nursery rhyme. After she was killed and her clinic destroyed, I never sang again. I don't know why I chose to now" she said. She see's the red light in the room reflecting in her glass. In her mind's eye she sees flashes of blood mixing with water running across the floor over her mother's barefeet as she approached the Security Forces that fateful day. She is no longer able to fight back the tears.

Bethlehem leans across the table and touches her hand. "Don't cry."

"I'm crying because I can see now what I could have been." Evolon responds without looking at him.

"It's not on you. It's in you. And what's in you, they can't take away. Maybe you just needed help to release what's trapped inside. Let me ask you this: Is a piano a stringed instrument or a percussion instrument?" Bethlehem leans in to this inquiry.

Evolon is perplexed by his odd question and ponders before replying "a piano has strings so I guess it's a stringed instrument.

"Most people do assume that. But we must look past the obvious. The top of a piano should be opened not just when its is being played. For if we take a long look inside the piano, we would see that the sound is actually being produced by vibrations initiated by hammers hitting the strings rather than by plucking or by moving a bow across them. Therefore, the piano is considered to be both a stringed instrument and a percussion instrument. Sometimes, the answer is not either or but both. In an argument, both parties can be right or both parties could be wrong. Embody the sum total of all that you are and all that you need to be. The door is unlocked. The ladder is down and the guards are sleeping" he declares.

They toast with her glass and his personal water container.

"To better days." Evolon is first to raise her glass.

Bethlehem is incapable of looking her in the eye without smiling "And to better nights."

As their eyes flirt with each other whether Evolon likes it or not, Bethlehem proposes yet another toast on the next shot. "To have nothing and still have something to lose" he says. His words are well received.

"To watermelons and sunflowers" Evolon adds.

"And to their seeds" Bethlehem has the final word.

Her body giving over slightly and finally entertains the lingering thought of the possible notion of their first night together with therapeutic screams. Normally, her emotions are effectively concealed but this night, or perhaps it was the alcohol, her beautiful eyes failed to honor their long held clandestine agreement. Noticing this, Bethlehem's eyes seemed to share even more info as an act of faith. Logic says never let go of her unless she lets go of you. Emotional intelligence says even then, go after her.

CHAPTER 5
ALWAYS PUSH

A single drop of water falls from the delicate petal of an exotic flower. A taste of sunlight translucencies the motion. The texture, form, size and shape are aesthetic characteristics of a master floriculturist tending to the various plants each with their own specific needs and requirements. All require proper drainage and benefit from the special Soylent green soil Nineveh provides from the decomposing bodies courtesy of its composting centers. In other cases, in addition to the microbes rich garden soil, sphagnum moss and an equal amount of sand usually produces the desired results for these delicate plants that require the heat regulation and the weather protection that Victorian glass greenhouses provides best. And of course, all the plants must be hydrated, in the appropriate amount and frequency, with distilled water or untainted rain water.

The ultimate Victorian greenhouses are always made of glass and not polycarbonates, which are a strong kind of plastic. One of the good by-products of an oil depleted society is the massive decrease of dependency on all plastics, especially single use petroleum plastics which even the Global Water Corporation banned the practice of in its production preference for glass. This held true in Nimrod's choice to stick to the classic horticultural glass. None of these choices express any explicit concerns for the benefit of the environment of course or to an even lesser extent, the higher cost of the expensive price. Glass is simply a very durable material and has a longer lifespan than plastic, more constant temperature, better light transmission, warmth absorption and offer a better control of humidity.

Here in the midst of this large classic glass structure with all the horticultural beauty it contains, stands the ugliness of the dreaded Nimrod. The tyrannical and murderous psychopath that used the Global Water Corporation to seize power during the greatest water crisis in the history of the world. His perfected disaster capitalism techniques and weaponization of water have become the citadel that now epitomizes the archetype of fascism. This grotesque monster with the kind of face that smiles have run very few miles across and even fewer are the moments he is able to briefly conceal his protruding horns. He now only appears to take the unassuming human form of a man that could pass as a mild mannered pharmacist providing pharmaceutical care to patients or as the master gardener in the white apron as he appears before us now, meticulously tending to his plants inside his expansive greenhouse that comprises nearly the entire east wing of the Palace.

Nimrod attends to his illustrious myriad of flowers, smelling them deeply, touching them gently and briefly, but he does not water them. He leaves that to the Gardners to labor. Who in addition to maintaining the proper sunlight, humidity, soil and temperature must also spray them with neem oil, a natural pesticide, and regularly wipe down the plants. Nimrod maintains the long held culture of the bourgeois and aristocratic encounters both inside the garden and out. Just like unrestrained capitalism, he is solely here to enjoy the fruits of their labor. He moves from item to item, first starting with his tulips, a favorite of the tyrannical Louis XIV, as some kind of twisted homage to the self-proclaimed Sun King. For Nimrod himself believed too, just like the Sun King, that all the Provinces of Nineveh revolved around him. But even the Sun King couldn't get his Birds of Prey to flower inside. Instead, they looked more like banana plants. Before he moves to the next items, he is careful to put on gloves before touching his collection of Digitalis.

These plants, also known as foxgloves, have several useful medicinal properties, but are extremely toxic if absorbed by the skin or ingested.

In fact, eating a foxglove can result in death by causing cardiac arrest. People have often confused foxglove with the relatively harmless Symphytum plant which is sometimes brewed into a tea, with fatal consequences. Symphytum could easily be mistaken for the deadly foxglove when not in flower because the leaves are very similar. However, the Symphytum leaves are untoothed, meaning they have smooth edges, whereas the foxglove leaves are toothed. Nimrod liked to call it the flower with more teeth than a Venus fly trap.

A humming bird buzzes by feasting on a variety of coral honey suckles. The world's smallest bird substitutes water with nectar and contributes to pollination which is the sole reason Nimrod tolerates them. As he moves on, he takes off the gloves when his cold eyes are displeased and the permanent frown on his stoic face deepens. His eyes have noticed some withering petals and limp stems of many of his other favorite items including his most prized hydrangea flowers. These flowers, when cut, will wilt and dehydrate easily. Therefore, they must remain in the soil which prevents them from being commercially shared or gifted which only serves to add to their intrinsic value. But even a wilted hydrangea may be completely restored by having its stem immersed in boiling water and its petals immersed in room temperature water. It is also because of this delicate balance and resilient quality that mostly attracted Nimrod to this particular variety of flowers as his favorite. He calls his gardener, Simele a large, but timid, soft and humble man that fears Nimrod for very good reason.

"Simele!" He shouts.

Simele rushes into to the area of the greenhouse where he was summoned. "Yes my lord?"

"Have you been over watering my flowers?" He demands to know.

"Why, no my lord. I have stuck to your exact instructions" he pleads sensing the impending danger.

"Then why are my flowers dying?" His rage now visibly confirmed.

"I do not know my lord. Perhaps they simply need a larger pot. I will retrieve one directly." Simele pleads in a vain attempt to buy him time and plot an escape route for he is now beginning to see the thunder and hear the lightning of the approaching storm.

Nimrod steps in his path and goes to the water source. He samples it with his index finger tip. He flashes a deadly look at Simele with piercing, fiery eyes after spitting on the floor as if he just tasted gasoline.

"This water is tainted! It is from the public supply!" He screams.

Simele begins to back away realizing too late that Nimrod stands between him and the door. In the doorway he spots Tiki, one of the house servants with a tray of lemonade shaking but frozen. Their eyes simultaneously greet and bear farewell. Simele licks his lips not out of thirst but of fear and has trouble swallowing and nervously wipes the beads of sweat that now appear across his forehead. He longs for the crow of a rooster for the signal of new day that will never come again. "But how could that be my lord?"

Nimrod violently murders Simele on the spot with a gardening tool to the neck. The blood spurting in time with his heartbeat has splattered across several flower petals as pots crashed to the floor in his fall. It is a brutal display of overkill as he has nearly been completely decapitated. Then Nimrod pages his security. They arrive quickly. They see Simele's lifeless body on the bloody floor now mixing with the top soil and the Soylent green fertilizer with spilled water behind Nimrod's feet and his eyes still wide open with reflections of the hydrangeas visible in his pupils. Nimrod is calmly wiping blood from his hands with a rag and removes a Cohiba Behike cigar and a cutter from his bloody apron and throws the rag and apron on the floor.

He meticulously sniffs the rare cigar as he sniffed the flowers before and runs it slowly under his nose as he inhales deeply with immense orgasmic pleasure. He cuts the short Cohiba and puts the cigar in his mouth and greets the awaiting lighter being held by the lead of the first Security Forces to arrive. He puffs like the proud father of a newborn apparently garnering pleasure and enjoyment from the deadly adrenaline rush after the brutal murder like a passionate sexual act with a messy clean up. After exhaling, he then addresses his security detail with eyes as cold as a shark taking stock of his surviving flowers "You know, men have lost their lives retrieving orchids from rocky cliffs. Even the thorns of roses have drawn blood. Now, someone has gotten to my garden's water supply. Find out who did. I want the best eagle eyes on this at all times until we get to the bottom of it. And get someone up here to clean up this damn mess!"

As he walks out the greenhouse, leaving a trail of bloody footprints, he passes a petrified Tiki still frozen with the tray of lemonade shaking in his trembling hands. Nimrod grabs a glass of the lemonade without missing a step in his stride beneath a large wood carving sign that sits above the door seal that reads Urna semper translation: Always push. On the floor mat below the words from the Sun King appear with a bloody foot print on the quote, 'I am the State.' Then a single drop of blood falls off the petal of an exotic flower on to the floor. A taste of sunlight reflected in Simele's lifeless eyes translucencies the motion in the coagulation pool of blood thickening around his body.

Now the intensity of the Security Forces have increased all over Nineveh. More check points, more drone surveillance, more boots on the ground, more raids and even street hustlers were harassed and jailed for selling solar distilled water. A group of children were even fired upon by an armed drone for using their slingshots. Fortunately, all the children were swift of foot and none of them were seriously injured. The Resistance was on the move. Security Forces kick in a door where a tortured informant provided a delayed tip. They secured the room. It was empty. The only thing present in the room was a table with a transistor radio broadcasting the still unknown Ndeble's voice from a pirate radio station during the failed raid.

"The system is like lions. We used to feed these lions with our fear and misery. Now with our self-disciplined resistance we are cutting off its food source. Hungry lions are far too weak to hunt its normal prey and will become more dangerous to humans. It will go out of its normal behavior and begin to raid villages."

Nimrod's initial responses were futile. So he considered a new approach, releasing weaponized nanotechnologies. Nanoscale robots the size of a mosquito could be programmed to use toxins to kill or immobilize people. His eager willingness to have them released on the Southside of Nineveh was only thwarted by the accurate counsel of Canaan, the head of the Security Forces, when he warned Nimrod that these early artificial life forms, having rudimentary intelligence to carry out programmed functions, along with the ability to reproduce made them a most dangerous liability. These autonomous bots ultimately would become self-replicating he cautioned. Rather, proposing another option, instead of their normal brutal assaults on illegal water harvesting solely, his notorious Security Forces turned to raiding every speakeasy in Nineveh.

They even raided the Nile Gallery but informants tipped the Resistance. Then their sinister focus was visited upon all those former violators who had avoided becoming repeat offenders. Canaan escalated tactics to incorporate interrogations by torture led by his own vicious but duplicitous tactics that to an extent actually fed the Resistance and proved to be beyond even his control as the efforts to deliver the intelligence Nimrod needed were stymied. Preventing this objective were the mouths of many people that had been wet by Ndeble and Evolon. So long they didn't dry, they didn't talk and the rain was falling. This is all that stood between the Resistance and the unleashing of Nimrod's full wrath and their annihilation.

A giant aquarium large enough to baptize a full grown man fills a luxurious penthouse suite. Looking through the tropical fish filled tank we can see Saisir on a waterbed engaged in a ménage à trois. They are not alone. Sitting in a massive leather chair, next to a beautiful sand glass standing erect upon a solid wood abstract end table, in the shadows of the room is Canaan. The well built Commander of the Security Forces with good posture and professional corporate air about him that has served him well in the ascension of his illustrious military career. He lights a cigar after he's seen enough. The action of closing the zippo lighter alerts everyone to his presence in the room. The women begin to cover themselves.

"What kind of cocking blocking shit is this?" Saisir demands to know half scared, half outraged.

"Get dressed and change your crypto currency drawers. Your father wants to see you." Canaan replies between slow cigar puffs.

"So what! He has my number." Saisir offers.

Canaan flips the sand glass and rises from the chair "You weren't answering the phone Saisir."

Before the sand runs out the conical glass, Saisir is now in the palace standing nervously in the presence of his brutal father that he knew all too well is capable of anything. Saisir attempts to take the initiative to plead his case and goes on the offense. He rushes to his father who is sitting in the parlor by a marble fire place under a life-sized oil portrait of King Leopold II. His ever presence Cohiba Behike burning in his hand with a crystal glass of fine red wine in the other.

"Father what is the meaning of this? Are we under attack?" He asks.

With the raging fire reflecting in his eyes he finishes his drink before responding.

"Yes we are, from within." He replies.

Saisir looks at Canaan who he sees smiling.

"Surely father you cannot possibly believe..." he begins.

"I believe that nepotism does not exist in this house" Nimrod responds still seated.

"But father!" Saisir exclaims.

Uncharacteristically, Nimrod continues to speak softly and calmly still looking directly into the fire as if he was consuming strength "Saisir, you know how it feels when you take a good shit? That's how it feels when you tell the truth. I know you don't have a malicious bone in your entire delicate body. When you were a boy, you were so scared of insects that someone could rob you with a centipede if they put it in your face. So I know whatever actions you took were not of evil intent. You take after your mother I am afraid. You are like the wilted petals of a hydrangea. Only able to withstand room temperature water to be revived. Whereas, I am the roots that can be immersed in boiling water and still thrive. So now that you are in hot water, just tell us who you gave the untainted water to and I will show your delicate, insect fearing, soul mercy."

He rises and approaches Saisir to look him directly in the eyes to put the fear into him. "Lie to me and I will castrate you!"

Saisir panics and falls to his knees holding on to his family jewels, for he knew his father was not a poker player and never bluffs. Bowing down to his murderous father's feet on Persian rugs and sobbingly begs for the most meaningful aspect of his life "I gave it to the Village Resistance Council! I'm sorry father! They threatened to feed me to the rats and put razors in my women's vagina!"

"Resistance Council? So there is an organized resistance that comes into my very home and dares to defy me?" Nimrod is utterly shocked and ponders his options as he turns away. He begins to pace the room like a caged animal. Breathing like a dragon with rapid cigar smoke filling the room until he finally freezes and fixates his eyes on Canaan. He replenishes his drink, sips and sits the glass down. "Saisir, you have sinned against our beloved Nineveh and disgraced your father. You must be punished. Take him to the dungeons" he orders.

Canaan immediately summons two members of the Security Force that lift Saisir off his feet.

"But father! You promised me mercy! Mercy father!" Saisir begs with futility.

"And so I shall. You should be eating rice with chopsticks with broken hands right now. But with the restraint and grace of my mercy you will simply remain there confined alone until the last Resister has been eliminated." Nimrod responds and dismisses him.

As Nimrod's men are forcibly taking Saisir away, he is struggling with them kicking and screaming before they finally drag him out, but not before he is able to continue to plead his case.

"Father no! No Father! Please! I beg of you! Don't do this! Please father! Must I free myself through death in order to please you? Can I at least get conjugal visits?" Saisir's desperate voice is heard long after being taken out the room.

Nimrod grabs his crystal glass and turns back to face the life size portrait of the monster he most admires. Standing before the fireplace, gazing into the eyes of King Leopold II as if to ask for monstrous guidance, he speaks nefariously to Canaan.

"You know, we are all are merchants of death, but unlike many other great predators in history, from Genghis Khan to the Spanish conquistadors, King Leopold never saw a drop of blood spilled in anger. He never even set foot in the Congo. Yet, he murdered more people than Hitler. But history paints Hitler as the colossal behemoth. There is something very modern about that. Like the bomber pilot in the stratosphere, above the clouds, or a drone pilot in a far off remote location playing a perceived war game while eating a snack, who never hears the screams or sees the shattered homes or the torn flesh. He never smells the bodies or undress in clothes bloodied and soiled by the carnage. Look into the eyes of motherless children. I am afraid, you and I do not have that luxury. All the tainted water in Nineveh couldn't wash away all the blood off our hands. Fortunately for us, most people only see the surface of things, but at the bottom of the Atlantic Ocean there lays a railroad track made of bones. 25,000 people died every day in Africa, Asia and Latin America for generations long before the World Water Crisis that enriched us began. They called that normal. They called that peace. They called that Western civilization."

He turns to face Canaan and takes a slow deep breath. "We are fighting and profiting from a war we did not start, but we did not come this far, just to come this far. The corpus plant is the largest flower in the world. It only blooms every 40 years, but when it finally does, it smells like rotten flesh. Do you know who these Resisters are?" He finally asks.

"As the light shines from the East, I will by the next full moon." Canaan answers.

"I don't care how many boreholes you need to

dig. If you must turn water to wine, find them and destroy them. I want to smell the corpus flowers early" Nimrod demands of him.

"Just as the mythical phoenix bird emerged from its ashes to soar gloriously thru the heavens. It will be done with pleasure my lord." Canaan submits.

He exits to leave Nimrod alone in angst. He pours himself another glass of Château Margaux and seats himself again by the fireplace beneath the life size portrait of King Leopold II above him with flames of the fire's burning reflection seen in the pupil of both of his eyes. He raises his glass to toast to the portrait "To man's inhumanity to man."

He needed that drink. He knew that tomorrow was the morning of the day of the beginning of things. He knew that an organized resistance, successful or not, was a signal that only served to confirm the existence of a group of dedicated people that were unafraid. Even Nimrod, the grotesque monster, knew that the true source of his power and his greatest weapon was the maintenance of the manufactured consent based mostly on fear. Without the maintenance of that institution of fear, he would soon begin to feel the very ground tremble the Persian rugs beneath his feet. For the first time in his adult life and most of his memory, he too was afraid. Afraid of what was possible. Even with his iron fist grip over the largest oasis in the world, he was conscious of the fact that no oppressor was invincible. He gulps the wine and proceeds to throw the unfinished drink in the beautiful crystal wine glass shattering into the fire. Knowing deep in his calloused soul, that his days left in power were now perhaps numbered.

That night, sleep didn't come easy. When the slow moving Sandman finally did arrive, he brought Nimrod the widower's deceased wife Cura to him in his dreams. A bittersweet nostalgia ran through his cold veins and rested upon the back of his closed eyelids. He could smell her perfume. He became aroused. His dream was so lucid. He could hear her voice speaking to him. He heard for the first time and comprehended the inaudible words she last whispered to him before she fell into a coma and eventually died. Her voice was subdued, but crystalline, "Some people are so poor, all they have is money." Nimrod screamed, awakening in a pool of hot sweat. He suffered the rest of the night with the onslaught of insomnia without the return of the Sandman. One of the most powerful men in the remaining world only found comfort on the other side of midnight in a tall glass of room temperature, untainted alkaline water and a new need for sleeping pills. The bully of the earth was just a man.

CHAPTER 6
HABBANIYA SQUARE

Nimrod, who now had a more focused target, made a call for all demons with well directed tenacity to relentlessly continue his repressive efforts through the dedicated and brutal Security Forces. The Resisters bold and defiant, continued to move like rivers through jungles, but in order to avoid open conflict have taken to traveling in smaller vehicles on side streets and alleys only. Finally, the inevitability of fate and blood arranges the confrontation when they each encounter the other in an alley cross section of the Southside of Nineveh called Habbaniya Square.

Habbaniya Square was the largest community market in Nineveh where goods were exchanged and bartered. The most popular items of course were unsanctioned food and untainted water. It represented the continuity of self reliance and communal responsibility in response to the economic reductionism that changed neighborhood food systems and resulted in massive supermarket closures except those controlled by the Global Water Corporation. Before the Water Crisis, only four corporations controlled the world's food supply. Now with the dearth of the world's bread basket, it was down to just one general store for all the slaves. Yet, community responsibility and government authority are both inadequate without the power and self-confidence that comes from owning productive capacity. In the old world of hegemonic culture, most of the skills of self-reliance were abandoned. But the hazard of a fascist regime's complete control over a community's life and work also gave rise to a situational awareness and necessity of collective local ownership that swung the pendulum. Therefore, Habbaniya Square the idea and not just the community market, had long been a point of contention for Nimrod and his Security Forces. It had to be crushed along with the Resistance.

And so it was. The third and final clandestine untainted water delivery fulfilling Saisir's treacherous commitment to the Resistance has been fulfilled. A portion of that delivery has just been made to a group of Resisters by Evolon and Bethlehem. They always chose the center of the square to camouflage their actions with the bustling market place as they would be encircled by rings of vendors. The outer rings were only those vendors whose wares were government sanctioned. Each inner ring became more and more illicit. The center of the ring functioned as an open-air illegal market. At the opportune time, a strategic series of vendors would move their stands to provide an opening for their exits and entrances. This operation was tolerated for a number of years due to corrupt Security Forces extracting payoffs, but Nimrod's fury has put an end to that. Now pulling away Evolon looks in her mirror and sees in her horror that Security Forces have begun to surround the men caught red handed with the blue gold contraband. She makes an effort to stop the truck to assist them and turnaround. Bethlehem grabs her hand and returns her attention forward.

"Forward ever, backwards never. Kwame Nkrumah" He offers the conciliatory remark. "There's nothing we can do for them now."

A line of Security Forces are approaching to cut them off. Evolon steps on the gas and runs over a number of them. Bethlehem drops an incendiary device out the window as a souvenir for the rest. Unfortunately, their comrades in the doomed faction of the Resisters are left to face their own rendezvous with kismet. Completely surrounded and kettled in with no possibility of escape, the ranking member of the Security Forces on site instructs his team to make a path for the Resisters and invites them to take advantage of his disingenuous offer to flee like a cat playing with a mouse.

"Aren't you even going to try to run?" He asks.

The first Resister to speak, looks him in the eyes and spits on the ground. "Fuck you! We never fold! If you haven't noticed yet we stop running a long time ago. Where we running to?"

The second Resister to speak puts some more respect on it with ten toes down. "And who we running from evil one? We ain't no track stars. Time's a wasting!"

The Security Force ranking member on site laughs and is joined by many of his men. "Brave men's souls. I presume you not going to tell us who the voice on the radio broadcast belongs to either? Very well then as you wish."

Just like wicked overseers on slave plantations that sought to instill fear in the hearts and colonized minds of the enslaved by making an example of not only of the captured runaway, but also of his pregnant wife, who was hung upside down by her ankles. Her womb cut open for the unborn to fall to the ground. Only to have the baby's head stomped in by the boots of the overseer for the entire captive audience on the plantation to see. Ensuring fear and obedience manufactured consent in the DNA memory of all that witnessed it and their unborn for generations to come.

He signals for his men to open fire and annihilates the entire squad putting them all down. Then they turn their sadistic guns on the fleeing crowds to make their point as clear as the Sharpeville massacre. Their bodies fall over each other as the same bullets pierce the valuable untainted 200 litre water tanks and mixes blood with the water that runs through the street over their boots just like it did over Assata's barefeet after committing an act of bravery with her own rendezvous with kismet.

However, despite this horror, Ndeble forever the chess player has cleverly planted false documents on all water deliveries alluding to a secret meeting to take place the morning of the next full moon. While the Security forces surveyed the scene the dead Resister's radio is playing Ndebele's own pirate broadcast.

"I would like to leave behind me the conviction that if we maintain a certain amount of caution and organization we deserve victory... you cannot carry out fundamental change without a certain

amount of madness. In this case, it comes from nonconformity, the courage to turn your back on the old formulas, the courage to invent the future. It took the madmen of yesterday for us to be able to act with extreme clarity today. I want to be one of those madmen."

–Thomas Sankara

"We must dare to invent the future. For whoever owns the water, owns you. This is the story of how a nation conquered the world and failed its people."

Unwittingly, the Security Forces take the bait and alert Canaan to the false information. Betrayal wears a pretty face. The great military strategist senses the Venus fly trap that has been set, but allows it to happen in a controlled environment selecting only the men he knew to be most loyal to Nimrod. This resulted in the ruination of the assigned platoon with absolute casualties on the part of the Security Forces due to having being drawn into the open in low ground whereas the Resisters were in a circular firing squad formation in an elevated covered position. The doomed Security Forces circled the bait of decoys in a truck loaded with empty barrels.

"Water, tainted or not, should not be wasted upon the ground like diarrhea eliminating precious fluids from the body and contributing to the dehydration of Nineveh" were the verbatim words of Ndbele's instructions.

With Canaan's primary objective achieved he now focused on the intel he needed to confirm the identities of the leaders of the Resistance as he watched the engagement from the safety of a small and loyal surveillance team armed with image stabilized binoculars with integrated 3D facial recognition. These tools revealed to him the identities of Ndbele and his beloved daughter Evolon. After annihilating the Security Forces, the blithe Resisters even chanted "Meri-Baal Lord of the Rebellion" in their ecstatic triumph injudiciously, but that was not necessarily a mistake on the part of Ndbele. Acts of war releases the raging bull in men. And once unleashed, that raging bull doesn't care if it's in a ring or a china shop.

With new information on the evening of the full moon, with a lot of fresh spilled blood, Canaan reports back to a well rested Nimrod self-medicated by sleeping pills. Who awaits him in a cashmere knitted bathrobe seated in an upright reclined position in a lounge chair on the poolside terrace being entertained by the talented hands of a beautiful harp player while listening to Edward Bernay's Propaganda audio book being read to him in front of a heated and lighted pool reflecting the cascading bright moonlit night on their faces. Canaan stands before him across a small table with freshly cut petunias between them.

"Greetings my lord." He begins.

Nimrod is stroking Aqua, his Koala bear pet sleeping on his lap that lives off the eucalyptus trees surrounding the pool. "You know the name Koala itself actually means no drink or without water? That's why I call her Aqua. She only requires the water content from the eucalyptus leaves. What news have you brought to me Canaan? Has the resistance been quelled?" Nimrod speaks without looking at him and ends the playback of the audio book and signals for the music to stop. The harp player exits quietly.

"The Resisters have all been eliminated." He reports falsely.

"Are you sure? I do not need to remind you that if an endless supply of untainted water were to reach the public it would awaken the minds of the masses and shake the very foundation of our power. Roses don't grow from concrete, but these are the seeds from wildflowers. They thrive through alternating rain and drought periods. Strong enough winds will carry them far and wide and make these weeds eventually uncontrollable. We can't afford to have them multiplying like the eggs of snakeheads or sunfish and grow to their fullest potential. We must be certain that this running faucet of subversiveness has been completely and permanently shut the fuck off." Nimrod turns to him.

Canaan looks down to avoid Nimrod's eyes that are now upon him.

"It is with a great cost of life to my men that I assure you my lord that we may now safely be rejoined by the company of your gentle son again." He continues the deception.

Nimrod rises with renewed vigor.

"Ahh yes! Then you must be truly convinced! Very well, good work Canaan. Would you care to join me for a swim?" He offers.

"I am afraid I have just eaten my lord." He replies.

"What did you have for dinner?" Nimrod inquires.

"I enjoyed the history of consciousness of one of the oldest organisms, Octopus. Shall I summon Sasir to be released?" Canaan asks.

Nimrod partially disrobes and begins to slowly descend into the heated pool.

"No. He can stand to go another night without

fornicating with the commons and their filth." He replies before submerging.

"As you wish my lord." Canaan responds with a crooked smile.

The lesser of two evils is still evil. The lesser evil is not in opposition to evil. It only makes way for a greater more proficient evil. The only thing more heinous than a vicious tyrant at the height of his power is the ambitious man that seeks to replace him. And what is unsought shall go undetected and least expected.

The next day Canaan personally arrives to the Angola dungeons of Nineveh to greet Saisir when he is released. Fully aware of the deplorable conditions in those dungeons where some men in order to survive resort to consuming their own urine and that Saisir was not afforded any comforts by his father beyond a larger ration of fresh water and the protection solitary confinement provided to prevent this gentle lamb from being fed to the wolves, he silently opens the limo door for him. Saisir, on the verge of a nervous breakdown in disheveled clothing, finds a small buffet of food, mini bar, a pretty woman with a smile, a sponge, a towel and a bucket of soapy water waiting to wash his soiled royal genitals and a fresh set of clothes.

Saisir is now fully enjoying the ride in the back of the limo patronizing the bar and receiving passionate fellatio after the girl's sanitary concerns are sufficiently satisfied to bring him back to life. After a sufficient amount of time, the tinted internal chauffeur's window comes down half-way with Canaan in the front passenger seat speaking to him while continuing to look straight ahead.

"You know we could have had you released last night. But your father wanted you to stay until morning." Canaan begins.

"Don't speak to me of my father! If I had the courage I would curse him to his face!" He mutters in near orgasmic satisfaction.

"You are a lover not a fighter Saisir, but you may very well have your chance to get back at him. There are a few Resisters still left. You do remember the sunflower Evolon don't you?" He reels him in.

Saisir is shocked at the news of this and ends his oral pleasure abruptly by pushing the girl aside "What! Not that bitch! She will come after me!" He exclaims. He then throws his soiled garments out the window and begins putting his fresh clothes on.

"Precisely, and when she does I will be there to greet her. These things I have spoken to you, you must not breathe a word of them to anyone. Do you overstand?" He explains.

"Sure, I overstand. That's why you brought me the food, the drink and the girl huh?" He asks.

Canaan adjusts the rearview mirror to make eye contact before speaking.

"You wouldn't have been able to hear me otherwise, would you?" He replies.

"I said I overstand. Now what?" He asks.

Canaan flashes a cold, sinister, reptilian look while still making eye contact with him in the mirror. The most Medusa aspect of Nineveh is that of a beast with two angels on its shoulders. One is no love. The other is no laughter. Rarely, do they ever disagree.

Next, the screaming woman and a bucket of dirty water are being thrown from the moving car into oncoming traffic. With her tumbling body being hit by a large truck and several cars that follow and quickly looks more like roadkill than the pretty young girl from moments before to Saisir's consternation. His eyes give firsthand witness testimony while Canaan never releases his cold reptilian gaze upon him.

"Take long walks in stormy weather or through deep snows in the fields and woods, if you would like to keep your spirits up. Deal with brute nature. Be cold and hungry and weary." Canaan declares to him.

"Henry David Thoreau" Saisir whispers through a trembling mouth reaching for the bar to replenish an empty glass with unsteady hands and frayed nerves.

"I see your father didn't waste his money on your formal education." Canaan continues to speak with his back turned.

"Yes, I am literate." Saisir retorts and throws his drink back. "The rich man is always sold to the institution which makes him rich."

"This is true" Canaan replies.

"Do you like horses Canaan?" He asks.

"I do" he responds knowing exactly where this is going.

"I heard you once took four horses and tied a man's limbs to each of them. You gave a verbal cue and they each ran in four different directions, quartering that man. You then riddle his still screaming torso to death with bullets" Saisir states his incredible charge emphatically.

"This is also true" Canaan shamelessly confesses.

"What I want to know is, what was the verbal cue that made the horses run?" Saisir asks.

"The greatest weapon of all and the name of your father's pet, Aqua" Canaan declares.

Upon hearing the name of his father's prized pet, he again recognizes his father's handiwork. They ride in a bit of silence before Saisir begins his own confession. "When I was a child, a dreamed of monsters. Usually, it was my mother that rushed to my room when she heard my screams to console and comfort me. But one night, my father came. He didn't console or comfort me. He asked me what scared me and what kind of monster it was. He said that fear of zombies means the fear of the masses. He said fear of vampires means the fear of the elite. I told him I didn't know what kind of monster it was because I always wake up when it grabs me. He then told me that monsters do exist, but they are too big to fit under my bed and far too few in number to be truly dangerous. More dangerous are the functionaries ready to believe and to act without asking questions. You sir, are one of those real life monsters."

"Indeed I am" Canaan confirms the obvious and turns to face Saisir. "But as your father's son, what then does that make you when the apple falls far from the tree?"

"I am not a monster" Saisir defiantly declares.

Canaan looks him up and down and smiles. "I know that." He returns facing forward and continues to speak. "I am simply saying that there are forces in nature that we don't understand, probably never will, that have influences on all of our lives that defies understanding. Even a fool can ask a question that a wise man can't answer."

Saisir is looking at a smear of blood on the car door and replies "A breathless soliloquy."

CHAPTER 7

UPSET THE SETUP

Evolon walks into a room where her father sits reading with Bethlehem close by doing the same. She greets both with her eyes when they look up and return to their reading briefly as she has a seat.

"Father I have just received word that Saisir has been released. Do you think your illustrious plan has worked?" She asks.

Both men close their books. Ndeble rises from behind his desk and walks around to lean against the front of it while pouring himself a cup of water before confronting his daughter. Bethlehem pulls out his pen and little notebook.

Ndeble begins slowly "We're still alive aren't we?"

"Are you about to tell me I told you so?" She submits.

Ndeble sips the water from his tea cup slowly, licks his lips and puts the cup down before responding

"You are my only child and I wouldn't dream of laughing at your expense. My work speaks for me, but yes, I told you so."

Bethlehem laughs and Evolon tries very hard to conceal another rarely seen smile that may not come again for a month of Sundays.

"Well, thank you for teaching me father the methods of a lightworker." She shakes her head softly.

Ndeble places his hand on his daughter's strong shoulder.

"When one teaches, two learn. Everything that happens to you is your teacher. The secret is to learn to sit at the feet of your life and be taught. Then you would not need a teacher to remind you because it would be written upon your heart." He explains while pausing momentarily to follow his daughter's diverted eyes to Bethlehem's writing. He returns to take his seat behind his desk. He takes another sip of water from his cup. "But as for now, we must not act. We do not yet know what is in play. Watch him for a few days and see who is watching him. Do not get too close and do not make a move, only watch Evolon. Remember, be water my child."

She rises from her chair and makes her way to the door before firing back over her shoulder "He's still alive isn't he?"

Evolon already knew exactly where to find the Prince of Nineveh fresh out the dungeons. Saisir was making up for lost time by partying at the Enchanted Garden, Nineveh's top club for the son's and daughters of the elite and their functionaries and subjects. The Enchanted Garden front exterior walls were covered with white Mandevilla flowerings. Its entire interior was completely white except for the black astro turf flooring in the seating area and the polished silver champagne buckets filled with Dom Perignon and Kona Nigari Water, one of the most expensive bottles of water in the world imported from Hawaii a thousand feet below the ocean surface. It was reserved for his birthday, but Saisir never saw the inside of a dungeon before so he broke it out early.

The Enchanted Garden's high ceilings had poles that descended to just above the head of the crowds that filled the space with blue light. In the center of the magnificent room was an elevated dance floor that made the crowd feel like they were on stage. The DJ table was an aquarium on a balcony overlooking the stage from behind the dance floor. The ceilings above the dance floor were without the descending poles of blue light. Instead, they featured skylights to gaze at the stars or howl at the moon. Most importantly for Evolon, the Enchanted Garden featured gigantic floor to ceiling windows and with it's all-white interior, even at night with only blue light illuminating the space, it was fairly visible from the outside.

This made it obviously all too easy for Evolon, the skilled hunter, to find her unassuming prey like apathetic sheep slaughtered in their sleep for their wool and their meat so that the thievery corporations' machines can feast. But alas, beware when the predator becomes the prey.

Evolon positions herself in an observation position on a building across the street. She uses the scope of her rifle on a hog saddled tripod as binoculars as she lays flat on the roof out of sight. She finds Saisir in a VIP terrace and struggles to resist the temptation of disappointing her father with her trigger finger as itchy as a dog infested with fleas.

Here she is approached directly by Canaan. She senses the unknown intruder's presence behind her by the pungent smell of cigar smoke. She relaxes her trigger finger. She raises her head from the scope and hears guns cock to indicate that the intruder is not alone. She freezes, realizing she's unable to return fire from this compromised position. She thinks of her father and becomes water.

"Before time and after time, there are those in strange lands that will always find the music. So, you are the great Evolon" Canaan begins.

"It's no love over here and we are beyond words" She is still startled but unafraid.

"Words always precedes war my dear, but I come in peace. To me an unnecessary action, or shot, or casualty is not only a waste, but a sin. I am Canaan. Perhaps you have heard of me?" He continues between cigar puffs.

"Well you can't be Nimrod's bloodhound Canaan or else I would be under arrest or dead" She responds.

"Well, you are half right, at least for now. It is true that I have served Nimrod and no you are not under arrest. And as you can see, you are still very much alive." He flirts with her as multiple red dots criss cross her body.

"I sleep on the floor with unclosed eyelids, so if I am not under arrest, then what the fuck do you want?" She demands.

"I want the same thing you want, Nimrod's head."

He confesses.

"To be replaced by yours I presume?" She quickly responds.

Canaan takes a long drag from his cigar. Exhales. Inhales. Taps ashes on the ground.

"Look, I am your bridge over troubled water, so lets not get into semantics, just try to focus on what we both agree on for now and that is change. My enemy's enemy and all that. Power is like a tiger, if you ride a tiger, you must be very careful when you get down, otherwise you find yourself inside the tiger's belly. But when things reach their peak, they decline. These are lessons before time and after time. What I would like to know are you interested in negotiating?" He explains trying not to lose his patience.

Evolon releases her initial tension and replies with a sense of righteous indignation "Negotiating yes. Compromising no."

"Very well then, at least that is a start. Nimrod now believes that your organization has been completely eliminated." He explains.

"Now why would he think that?" Evolon awaits the punchline.

"Because I told him that to buy you time to replenish the numbers you lost in Habbinya Square. A sign is not the real thing. It points to the real thing. You are not yet strong enough to defeat Nimrod's army head on. That is why your father has focused his attention on his weakness, which is his son, Saisir." He explains further.

At that very moment, Saisir is doing what he does best, parlaying with several beautiful, thirsty women throwing champagne in the air after popping bottles and pouring it all over them.

"Yes, he is truly pathetic. Still playing like a child on the playground during recess" Evolon is lured in while ambidextrously still observing Saisir briefly so not to lose track of him.

"Indeed, he is. I am afraid you can't turn a lady bug blue. But he is a trusting lamb. Just another angel with a dirty face. And as long as he has hatred for his father, Nimrod is vulnerable. You are here in hopes of capturing more untainted water, I am here to inform you that Saisir is more valuable than you think" said Canaan.

"How valuable?" Evolon is beyond intrigued.

"A rolling stone gathers no moss, but it gains a certain polish. He is worth more than his weight in blue gold or that of a fuel rod portable charger" he declares.

"How so?" She demands to know.

"Saisir is the designer of the only water purification system that removes the contaminant. Why do you think Nimrod keeps him around? Because he loves him? He doesn't ever want to have Saisir share what he knows with anyone, but he cannot very well afford to eliminate him out of fear he may need him someday. Now, with this knowledge you could build an army. Only then could you have the hopes of facing Nimrod or be left to commit acts of bravery like your beloved mother did." Canaan drops the mic.

She is infuriated by the mentioning of her mother and finds it again difficult to maintain her composure. A true marksman, she knew she could quite possibly get off a kill shot to take Canaan out, but the red dots criss crossing her torso reminded her that if she did so, she would in fact, be simply committing another act of bravery before joining her mother just like Canaan described. He was testing her. She remembers Bethlehem's words 'The first thought is the spirit. The second is the mind.' She composes herself. She remains water, hot water, but water nevertheless. "True spit? Still water runs that damn deep, huh? You mean that little piece of shit all this time? Is this real or not? The beast got to be dropped."

"A primal objective I am sure, but you can only take out demons in your range. You are fearless, but don't be careless. Do you want untainted water for your people or do you want revenge?" Canaan responds.

"Why should I take your word for all this?" Evolon asks.

"You shouldn't. You must use both sides of the blade. So you should rather use your freedom to take this message back to the Meri-Baal. There are too many winding roads ahead for speeding. You are the young feisty warrior and you need to confer with the old scholar. He is old and wise but not tired and disappointed. He will know what to do. You will have my unseen assistance. The future belongs to those who believe in the beauty of their dreams, my dear. Now, until then, I bid you farewell" Canaan departs as a soft drizzling rain begins to fall on the just and the unjust alike, leaving Evolon to ponder their smart and serious conversation and continue to observe Saisir with more restraint, but with renewed eyes of interest.

She resumes her sniper position using her scope

as binoculars, but with her finger off the trigger this time.

"And to think, I almost killed you. My father is indeed prophetic" she mutters to herself thinking of Bethlehem's words.

We now find the Meri-Baal in a room surrounded by children. A beautiful little girl is doodling and not paying much attention.

"Khepera would you like to repeat what I just said please?" Ndeble asks.

The little girl is frozen like a deer in headlights.

"I am sorry Baba" she apologizes.

"Listening is a what?" Ndeble asks the class.

"A skill" the children respond in unison.

"Are you developing it?" He asks gently taunting Khepera.

"No" the children reply.

"As I was saying, our bodies are comprised of over 70% of water. The earth's surface is also covered with over 70% of water. Our molecular structure has atoms that rotate like the earth on its axis and like the planets around the sun. We share 50% of our DNA with trees. Therefore, in our tardy, but sincere efforts to create a naturally sustainable system we must recognize that earth and man are inextricably intertwined. Our brains even operate like lighting in a bottle. That is why we refer to a good thought as..." he submits the leading question.

One of the children raises their hand to answer before being acknowledged.

"A bright idea" the child proudly responds.

"Yes indeed my child, yes indeed. That will be all for today. Next week we will study the ancient clay tablets of the Ashurbanipal. Peace to the ancestors" Ndeble concludes.

"And those that are doing the work!" The children and Evolon respond in unison.

Children in war zones are often deprived of receiving an education. They increasingly face risks of early marriage, child labor and recruitment into armed groups. The Meri-Baal, the former teacher, recognized this and made a personal commitment to continuing their education despite the ongoing conflicts around them. He recognized that the youth, just like water, were an invaluable asset. There is a sacred relationship between children and elders.

Little Khepera hands Evolon the picture she was drawing instead of listening to her father. She bends her knees to stoop down so to meet the child on her eye level and see's it is a picture of her.

"I hope you like it." Khepera says.

Evolon forces a smile "I like kids' work more than work by professional artists any day. Thank you little one. May you become the blessings our ancestors have prayed for."

Khepera smiles and joins all the children as they exit with Evolon waiting to speak to her father. She dances pleasurably with the nostalgia in the room as she fingers the desks and reminisces of the fond memories from her childhood before tragedy struck.

"I see you haven't changed much" she whispers.

She walks over to the window and observes the children now on the playground below chanting the classic nursery rhyme beneath the silk cotton tree that provides shade in the plaza and stuffing for mattresses and pillows. They are engaged in a tinkling dance. The children weave through rapid moving parallel pairs of bamboo poles with bare feet and ankles. The poles are used as percussive instruments and are held by other children sitting or kneeling. They produce clapping sounds as they are struck against the ground in a triple meter pattern. The poles are tapped twice on the ground on the first two beats, then brought together on the third beat. The children dance carefully following the rhythm so as not to get their feet or ankles caught between the poles as they snap closed. The tempo of the bamboo poles becomes faster as the dance progresses, forcing the dancers closer together as their movements become more frantic. The dancers hold hands at the last part of the dance, when the tempo is the fastest. They end the dance by letting go of each other's hands and stepping out entirely of the moving bamboo poles. While they dance, they recite the nursery rhyme known by all the children in Nineveh. She mouths along with them, "Water, water everywhere, not any drop to drink." Her father smiles quietly and proceeds to clean up the classroom behind the children.

"I believe I moved a lot faster when you sat in this room. And public education is still the most powerful institution on the planet. If our youth learn how to think, no one can tell them what to think. Those who control the education of children..." Evolon finishes her father's statement.

"Control the future. But I think god and the devil are playing with our souls" still looking out the window.

Concluding his menial chores and observing his daughter directly.

"Angels and demons are always at play. What, you have never been to a funeral and a wedding on the same day before? If we give our children sound self love they will be able to deal with whatever life puts before them. But you sound troubled my dear, even more than usual. What have you seen?" He asks.

Bethlehem enters the room with a new bounce in his step restraining a smile. The kind of smile that makes other people wonder what you've been up to or perhaps one a mischievous child may have after they finally get what they wanted. This is an outturn due to the fact that he was summoned by Evolon after her near brush with death in the too close for comfort encounter with Canaan the night before that brought his unrequited love to an end. In her vulnerable emotional state, she experienced the most unlikeliest of aphrodisiacs, surviving death. Now that she was outside her comfort zone, she could think of no better way to show the ancestors her gratitude for still being alive than throwing herself into Bethlehem's awaiting arms. Her epiphany was the realization that comfort is the poison and nothing good can grow from there. So she decided to finally submitted to his advances and fervidly consummated their seemingly inevitable and clandestinely arranged relationship in a soft drizzling rain with no words spoken.

It was apropos that it took place on the very same rooftop on the very same night where she almost wasted Saisir's life and possibly that of Canaan's himself, if she was able to succeed in getting a shot off that found its mark. Nevertheless, she most certainly would have surely sacrificed her own life in an act of futile bravery as clearly confirmed by the red dots that crisscrossed her head and torso at the time of Canaan's foreboding reference to her mother. The eternal fire of her rage that can consume anything, fortunately did not consume her. She put water to fire. In her awakening, where emotions make good servants but poor masters, she called her more than willing devoted companion Bethlehem because her spirit chose that now near sacred location on that night of thorns and rose petals to plant her own garden and to thank him for convincing her of the divine wisdom that misery is only optional. Finally freeing her warrior soul that was unafraid to die, but too afraid to live and love.

"The king has no loyal subjects" he announces.

"Really? The Emperor wears no clothes. Do tell" Ndeble is intrigued.

Evolon makes her way to her father's ever present tea cup and pours herself a cup of water. Instead of gulping it down like she normally does, she sips it slowly like it's hot tea like her wise father and takes a seat in her old desk before she begins.

"I was approached directly by Canaan the head of Nimrod's Security Force last night. He knows our identities. He says that your prized nymphomaniac is actually the only one who knows how to remove the contaminate from the water" she shares with an exhale.

Ndeble rubs his beard.

"I see, this is precisely the way opener we have been waiting for!" He declares.

"But father, how can we trust his forked tongue?" Evolon inquires.

"Because he approached you himself. The great Sun Tzu taught us 'If you know the enemy and know yourself you need not fear the results of a hundred battles.' If he had sent a proxy, I would then be suspicious. But by exposing himself directly to you he took the risk of being eliminated himself and refused the opportunity to capture our most powerful warrior. If you did not trust him, why did you not kill him or him you?" He challenges her.

"I do not know" Evolon responds in a rare moment of feeling unsure of herself.

"Ahh! You are at last learning to harness your power by listening to that little voice within you. In the core make-up of every human being lays the embodied possibility for acts of astounding compassion and magnanimity or acts of horrific and seemingly unsurpassable evil. In our formative years, these capacities are accessed, and the 'innocent' games of childhood become the life-giving or death-dealing maneuverings of adult life. You obviously both had subconsciously recognized that wars are poor chisels for carving out peaceful tomorrows." Ndeble provides a monologue for Bethlehem notebook.

"But father, what if we are wrong!? We will be facing the elimination of the Resistance with this prostituted alliance. We should not compromise with evil to renounce the mandate of hope given to us by the people of Nineveh. This is after all, Canaan we're taking about. Even if his word are true, his motives are not and are surely as fake as South African Apartheid prison suicides." she cautions.

"The heart is like grain, we are the mill. If the mill doesn't turn, what will the baker do?" Ndbele quotes the 13th century Persian poet Rumi from a popular passage that his daughter learned well under his tutelage.

"The body is the millstone, water is thought" she replies with exasperation and heavy sighes.

"And...?" Ndbele poignantly inquires again.

"Stone says: Water knows what the story is" Evolon reluctantly responds.

"Do you remember my favorite film?" Ndbele asks.

"The Battle of Algiers" Evolon replies with an inquisitive response.

"Yes. It's hard enough to start a revolution, even harder to sustain it, and hardest of all to win it. But it's only afterwards, once we've won, that the real difficulties begin. Therefore, until then, we have neither permanent friends nor permanent enemies, only permanent interests. Surely, he has his own nefarious interests, we will deal with him when the time comes, but for now our current interests are better served by acting upon this information rather than ignoring it. Even if it comes from a perfidious source. Always remember that even a broke clock is right two times a day. The true test of knowledge is the proven capacity for action. Craziness is not always an act. Sometimes, not to act is craziness. Besides, as you say, he knows our identities. We have no choice. We must move cautiously, but we must move. Balancing self preservation with our collective responsibility. For every advantage, there is a disadvantage. For every disadvantage, there are two advantages. So if you can't take advantage, take disadvantage. Now, where is Saisir?" He asks.

"He is in the penthouse suite at the Taj Mahal in the northern quadrant. It will be very difficult to get to him there" Bethlehem accurately reports.

Evolon produces a tracking device. "There is always something that can be done. We'll just have to wait for him to move" she offers a solution.

"Have you ever noticed that the hardest thing to do and the right thing to do are often the same thing?" Bethlehem inquires.

"I think you should stick to writing, Baba Jr" Evolon playfully jabs at him.

Ndeble, a master of reading people, takes great personal satisfaction in knowing that his subversive intentions of finding a suitable mate for his beloved daughter has finally proven to be successful.

"Influence is a science" Ndeble suddenly declares as an intellectual challenge.

"Passion is a fruit" Evolon affirms.

"Work is a discipline" Bethlehem concludes.

A mutual smile of a family bond is silently established with all in a brief moment of silence. It was as if the symbolically mental giving away of a daughter to a husband at a wedding the father would happily pay for but because of the cruel irony of fate would never take place.

"You are both great students. Warriors and scholars but we must study and understand the points of danger. I saw a mural today. It was of six women embracing each other and the words said, 'All or nothing.' I have been pondering the meaning of that all day" Ndeble confesses.

"What does that mean to you?" Evolon asks.

"Well, with women being the symbol of life and six being the symbol of death, I think it is a significant visual analysis of the beauty of our struggle or perhaps the coming of life and the simultaneous lost of life. Angels and demons are always at play" he replies with a glare of caution while replenishing his tea cup.

Bethlehem closes his little book of numbers and shakes his teacher's hand looking him directly in the eyes. Evolon kisses her father's free hand and they both depart leaving him for the evening.

Bringing all the force of his humanity, passion

and clarity to bear, Ndeble now ponders the bright hopes and cynical betrayal of revolution. He is discomforted by the thought of all the front-line fighting and euphoria. Truth be told, propaganda and distortion are perpetrated by both sides as he finally and reluctantly admits to himself in thought. His top priority now was pondering the end game of how to prevent the tragic collapse of the inevitably successful revolution dissolving into warring factions amongst themselves. But he releases an unrestrained smile when he is left alone long enough with his prized framed picture retrieved from his desk of his deceased beloved wife Assata and is comforted by the thought of the potential promise of an eventual grandchild while mourning the impending lost that he has now sensed is also sure to come. "Mothers' stories are long in telling, are sometimes filled with silent echoes of resonances beyond their children knowing" he speaks out loud to his wife.

He finishes the water in his ever present accoutrement, his prized tea cup, a treasured gift from Assata. He rises to replenish his cup but this time he goes into his locked cabinet and reaches to retrieve a bottle of Origin Bitters, an elixir and spiritual drink with herbal extracts, that is reserved only for special occasions. He laments with the guilt of his role as a father, husband and protector. He wrestles with his subconscious and wonders again out loud to his deceased wife. "You know how I used to be very annoyed by clocks that ticked loudly? I guess just like the taste buds of our childhood has changed, so has my way of thinking. I now fully appreciate the sound of every ticking, fleeting second. It is a precious and beautiful thing... What kind of man sends his only daughter off into battle after failing to protect her mother and his wife?" He bemoans the conclusion, but finds some warmth in the perceived response from his wife when the answer immediately comes to him. Those who will not risk cannot win. He lights a spliff and sips from his cup to numb the pain and the shame of his culpability. Before he even realizes it, a tear falls from his left eye and slowly trickles down the side of his face landing slowly in the tea cup. Throwing caution to wind he mutters, "Vengeance is mine if I ever was to lose her" slips from his quivering lips of guilt with much righteous indignation, "but if we make it out of this, it would be one hell of a story to tell the children. I just need a louder clock" as the forever grieving widower raises his tea cup to toast to the image and memory of his cherished wife with his face buried in his free hand "To another day."

Moments later, his security detail, that was waiting outside for quite sometime during his intimate reflection, now enters the room to transport him home safely.

CHAPTER 8
PUBLIC INTEREST DOCTRINE

Man plans and God laughs. Life is so unpredictable and unexpected changes will inevitably occur. In spite of possible calamities, we are urged to think positively and maintain a spirit of optimism by not dwelling on the negative possibilities. We try as we may to minimize the possibilities of negative things happening to us or our loved ones. Putting on our seatbelts, wearing helmets, regularly monitoring what we put into our bodies and of course, avoiding confronting danger head on at all cost. But deep down we realize we can't always avoid disastrous acts of fate or that of Mother Nature. We can't prevent all accidents from happening or even keep our loved ones safe at all times. Ndeble knew this all too well. He knew that despite his meticulous planning, methodic preparations, it all boiled down to the simple notion, that the fate of the entire Resistance laid with him winning the final debate with Saisir to convince him to take the final step in betraying his father. Either he will betray his family or that of another family. Aware of the obvious dysfunctionality of Saisir's family, Ndeble was betting on the latter that blood was not thicker than water with the full knowledge that some men cannot be persuaded.

They await for Saisir's motorcade to move in the Northern Quadrant. They have already managed to clandestinely overtake his driver before he even gets in the car with the blind eye assistance of Canaan. As the small motorcade continues a truck temporarily blocks the view of Saisir's security tailing them to avoid a sink hole long enough for them to stop to let Ndeble get in undetected by the security team and now Evolon turns around behind tinted windows pointing a sawed off shotgun resting on top of her forearm that rest across the back of bucket seats with no head rest. The safety is still on as it points eye level at Saisir's head from the front seat. Bethlehem is driving.

"Do you remember me Saisir?" She asks.

"Fuck... not you again!" He gasps looking around for his unknowing security.

She removes the shotgun when her father enters the backseat forcing Saisir to slide over.

"Don't shit your pants pretty boy. We just want to talk, for now." She says.

"About what? I no longer have any access to my father's private water supply. My untainted water access is as dry as the Zayandeh Rud River. If I knew you were coming I would have saved you a few bottles of Kona Nigari Water from my party" He says sarcastically.

"We are not interested in dead rivers or what you can't do. You can't fight change" Ndeble tells him.

"Look, I told you it would ruin the fucking flowers. I went to the dungeons because of you! I bore the burden of your dreams. Our business here is done. What else do you want for me?" Is his exasperated claim.

Ndbele looks directly at him. "What I want to know from you is simply this. Which is more important? Science or philosophy?"

Without even pausing long enough to ponder the ancient old question Saisir quickly blurts out erroneously without thinking first. "Science of course, it is the foundation of facts that describes everything."

Just like I thought Ndbele surmises. "There would be no science without philosophy. I mention this to draw attention to a deeper point, all of human knowledge has grown out of philosophy; the 'mothership' of science, economics, mathematics, politics, everything. It is both logic and emotional intelligence. We need both. Otherwise, men can starve from a lack of self-realization as much as they can from a lack of bread. Or do you plan to go to your grave with the knowledge of the only water purification system that removes the contaminate that controls the minds of the people of Nineveh and prevents them from rising up against Nimrod?"

Saisir looks out the window and pauses at the revelation. He realizes this is the work of Canaan but unsure as what to do or what to say. So he told the truth. "My father has more money than there are ants left on earth. He would destroy me and this entire city before he would allow anything but just that to happen."

"Sometimes, the drummer leads the band. We are called to be architects of the future; not its victims. And the best way to predict the future, is to create it. What will you do when nothing else matters Saisir? After your father's misrule is over do you plan to be buried with him like all the other slaves of the great Pharaohs of Kemet?" Ndbele makes his case.

A frustrated Saisir turns to confront him "Why don't you people get it? Your little auspicious schemes will never work! My nefarious father has put in place a contingency plan for every imaginable variable that would threaten his power. He even monitors waste water analysis from a variety of sources to alert him before tainted water consumption falls below critical mass efficacy levels. There is nothing you can do to defeat his army! Canaan knows you are here and you probably will be left to burn in the streets long before me!"

"Limitations are for people who accept them Saisir. You are stuck in your own reasoning and I understand if my heart is more powerful than your mind can comprehend at this moment. But you look like a man who has been pushed to the point of losing his purpose. A life without a purpose is a life filled with vices to try to fill the bottomless holes created by that emptiness. A 40 liter bucket carried around your neck like an albatross. 'His eyes flash momentarily to catch Evolon's in the rearview mirror to stress the significance of his double entendre.' A particle scheme, as you say, is either one already in existence, or a scheme that could be carried out under the existing conditions; but it is exactly those existing conditions that we object to. Any scheme that could accept the existing conditions is both wrong and foolish. The true criterion of the practical, therefore, is not whether the latter can keep intact the wrong and foolish;

rather it is whether the scheme has the vitality to leave the stagnant waters of the old, and build, as well as sustain life" Ndbele lectures.

"I'd rather make sense, than history. Without an army, your poetic words of spiel are simply beautifully absurd" Saisir is still unmoved.

"Oh ye of little faith. It's true, war has rarely meant freedom for our people. But the greatest power is convincing people that they don't have any. You are simply blinded by your own mortality and fear. Your silence will not save you nor will an armor of your fear protect you. During the course of a man's life, if he doesn't find something he is willing to die for, then he is no longer fit to live. You cannot be neutral on a moving train. The laws of inertia forbids it Saisir. Our survival has been due to our ability to rise up against the forces aimed at destroying us. Our mere existence is a victory. Everyday something or someone has tried to kill us and has failed. We are not here because of the system; we are here in spite of the system. With unlimited access to fresh, untainted water, we can build an army. You are now an unique occurrence of which you are the most reliable measure of all the possibilities." Ndbele's lecture continues.

"Even if I helped you, after the time it would take

for the affects of the contaminate to wear off and even longer for the contaminated water supply to be replenished and distributed to the point to even have the hopes building such a lucid army would be too late. By that time your plan would be exposed and we would all be dead, burned alive in the Southside streets of Nineveh! It is of no use!" Saisir is now wrestling with the concept in his mind and all Ndbele has to do is to convince him of a way out somehow.

"If you are not focused, you don't have anything. Did you know that nearly every slave rebellion in the Americas was thwarted by a slave? Primarily because of the meritorious manumissions that promised any slave their freedom if they revealed any seditious plans of others. But whenever the slaves get together, Pharaoh cannot hold them in bondage. The slave owners knew this. Because they knew that nothing can stop a man with the right mental attitude from achieving his goal; likewise nothing on earth can help the man with the wrong mental attitude. You cannot put a rope around the neck of an idea; you cannot put an idea up against the barrack-square wall and riddle it with bullets; burn it alive, you cannot confine it in the strongest prison cell your father's slaves could ever build. And it does not require a majority to prevail, but rather a critical mass, an irate, tireless minority to set brush fires in the minds of the people" Ndbele's debate mastery is prevalent.

"And fire to their asses" Evolon interjects adjusting the review mirror.

"Global water consumption doubles every twenty years. This problem is only going to get worse. In our every deliberation, we must consider the impact of our decisions on the next seven generations. The optimist sees opportunity in every danger; the pessimist sees danger in every opportunity. Time plays no favorites and will pass whether you act or not. The system moves no further than it is gently pushed or violently dragged. All of your doubts are man made and therefore changeable by acts of man and sheer human will. Your fear of death creates the very chains of your bondage. All of us are walking in the same direction." Ndeble asserts.

"What lies before us all, but the open grave." Bethlehem mumbles to himself while Evolon smiles to herself and discreetly squeezes his hand.

"A different world is not only possible Saisir, it is also necessary. Man doesn't know what he is capable of until he is asked or pushed. I am both pushing and asking Saisir. Once you are really challenged, you find something in yourself. We must be as armed with knowledge as our adversaries. But imagination is more important that knowledge, so if you don't believe in the possibility of the impossibility, you will never be free." Ndbele's words have finally found their mark.

Another truck blocks the view of Saisir's security detail momentarily as a decoy vehicle planted a spike in its tire path. The car stops and Ndeble upon exiting turns and speaks his last parting words.

"Saisir, allow me to recapitulate. You have a lifestyle, not a life. And that bridge leads to nowhere. Change does not roll in on the wheels of inevitability, but comes through continuous struggle. So we must straighten our backs and work for our freedom. A man can't ride you unless your back is bent. You are spiritually war torn. So please, get rid of that 40 liter bucket around your neck and stand up. It's time for healing. Your position is pivotable. There are people who didn't like their birthdate on the Greco-Roman calendar. So they changed their birthdate by simply choosing a more favorable time of the year to celebrate their birthdays in warmth. The greatest power is convincing people they don't haven any. And power is the awareness of the fact you have power. So, whatever you decide to do remember this, there are special people and unfortunate people. The trick is to know which one you are and act accordingly. Don't die with words in your mouth and go home and do nothing. A hopeless man is a dead man. And we all are hoping you have the courage to do what needs to be done. There is no problem we are unable to resolve" Ndbele won the debate.

He is then immediately picked up by another car and traffic resumes slowly after navigating around the disabled vehicle. Evolon turns around and again points the shotgun still on safety at Saisir's face, but this time he appears to have no fear. He looks blankly at her, lost in his own deep thoughts and ignoring the presence of the gun like someone who has been robbed too many times before. Desensitized from the repeated threats of violence, even the meek will eventually become braver in the face of adversity.

"So, what will it be? Go with god or come with me?" Evolon asks. Her words sound like a dream state to him.

Saisir is triggered mentally. He is reminded of his childhood with something his mother used to say to comfort him each and every time after he had his long recurring nightmare. As a child, he would dream of being immobilized in his bed by the fear of an approaching monster. He was unable to move or scream. He could hear the lurking monster in the dark getting closer and closer. The heavy breathing. The thunderous footsteps vibrating. He could even see his blood red eyes glowing in the dark as they approached. But it wasn't until the very moment the monster grabbed him that he was released from the fear of his nightmare and awakened. His mother would always rush to his side after hearing his horrid screams. She would comfort him gently in her arms, rocking him and say and force him to repeat "We must face our fears. We gain strength, courage, and confidence by every experience in which we stop to look fear in the face. Nightmares are our dreams training us all to face our fears."

The last time he had such a nightmare and his mother rushed to his side just as quickly as she had done dozens of times before and after she patiently forced him to repeat that same affirmation she added something else that he hadn't thought about again until that very moment. She said, "To hope is to dream and power is how much we believe we can make those dreams reality. Hope and power together are a measure of your ability to affect change and to create your ideal future. Hope is to dream. And if the future you are dreaming doesn't look like the present you are constructing, then you should look more closely. Be brave my son. Be brave." Then she kissed him for the very last time.

"Go with god or come with me?" Evolon now impatiently repeats her self as his dream state fades.

"I shall go with you, of course and face my fears. I only hope that the future will not be indifferent to me. But, we are all going to die" he said.

She smiles, removes the loaded gun on safety and turns back around in her seat.

"You just now realizing that?" She snaps back. "Sometimes, making a better future simply means saying no to the present. Besides, what lies before us all, but the open grave?"

"We are all traveling in the same direction." Bethlehem adds.

Evolon and Bethlehem's eyes lock and rare smiles are exchanged. She then looks into the rearview mirror at Saisir who continues to look out the window.

"Now that you know, what will you do with your wheelbarrow of soil?" She challenges him to ponder the thought further.

"Not everything that is faced can be changed, but nothing can be changed until it is faced" Saisir thinks out loud.

"What do you know about James Baldwin boy?" Evolon is surprised.

"I do read, thank you very much." Saisir snaps back indignantly.

"It is beginning to rain. This is a divine sign." Bethlehem concludes.

The normal cause celebre ensues in Nineveh with the people flooding the streets for the elusive and invaluable contraband of rainwater. Bethlehem carefully navigates the car slowly through the exhilaration of the crowds flooding the streets collecting bowls of water carried on their heads, bathing, washing clothes, brushing their teeth and of course, with the most exuberant ones even dancing in the rain in between upside down umbrellas. As the down pour begins to lighten, a bright rainbow appears as the setting sun breaks through the clouds for a few last breathtaking moments. The car continues to navigate the flooded streets in the general direction of the end of the rainbow as if they were all in search of a pot of gold.

Roman Emperor Justinian in 528 A. D. Introduced the Public Trust Doctrine that asserted that common resources such as water are to be held in trust by the state for the use and enjoyment of the general public rather than private interests. He further stated, "By the law of nature these things are common to all mankind; the air, running water, the sea and consequently the shore of the seas." His prophetic words alluded to the coming of war over water and possibly, with the advent of the necessary technology, the coming war over the air.

CHAPTER 9

THE CONTAMINANT

The Resisters surround a large round table as Saisir prepares to explain the details of the purification process and include them in the circle of knowledge. Bethlehem pulls out his notebook and the Meri-Baal pours rainwater from the pitcher and slowly sips his water from a tea cup.

"Okay pretty boy tell us, how does this thing work?' Evolon is impatient and first to speak.

"Well, first of all, the contaminant is actually an enzyme that attaches itself to the molecules of the water by an activant. As you know, boiling and distillation alone will not remove it. What you need is a non-bacterial, readily biodegradable enzymatic soap solution for..." Saisir begins.

"A what?" Evolon asks for clarity.

"Basically an enzyme cleaner with peppermint." Saisir elaborates.

"Wouldn't that make the water hazardous to drink?" Ndbele puts his tea cup down.

"Yes and it will irritate the eyes and the skin too, so do not touch or drink this solution" Saisir said.

"So we must first poison the water like in the Mosul Diaries? Then in order for us to make it safe?" Evolon said.

"Well, there is a certain level of entropy involved yes, but we must move from trauma to innovation. We can turn waste water into drinkable water, but the drugs and medicines would remain. It's a picayune amount 1 decilitre per litre. Just like the algal blooms first poisoned the water that created the peak of this crisis we must design a method to reverse engineer this. It will work. In fact, you should wear gloves. The cleaner will simply inhibit the enzymes that act as a variant of gamma hydroxybutyric acid" Saisir said.

Everyone leans in and looks on inquisitively for more clarity.

"The date rape drug?" Evolon asks.

Saisir is surprised by her revelation, but not her father who smiles slower than he sips his water.

"Yeah, that's right. You thought all those beautiful

thirsty girls loved me? This is the active ingredient, albeit in a mild form, that pacifies your people and enriches my adventurous sex life" Saisir explains.

"You mean your remorselessly promiscuous, pathetic ass life." Evolon said.

"Hey, look I am trying to help you people so..." Saisir says before being cut off.

Evolon turns in a leather swivel chair to face him with the long slit in her dress revealing the .45 strapped to her leg and eyes of fire. Saisir notices for the first time the chain around her neck with a half cent coin as an ornament.

"Why are you wearing a half cent coin around your neck? I thought they stop making those generations ago" Saisir remarks with a glimpse of bravery.

Evolon leans in and lowers her voice "Because I am the lowest common denominator. I can't be broken down any further. I have reached my limit. Like I have reached my limit with you."

"Please just stop judging me" Saisir continues.

"Boy, put down the champagne! The poor remembers. The rich forgets. There is a price to be paid for all the water you played with. Have you ever once thought of the amount of lives that have been lost while you were running around here playing Hugh fucking Hefner on a king sized water bed surrounded by aquariums while people couldn't even afford to put water on the table?" Evolon is heated and demands to know now.

"Evolon, please. He is here now. A contrite presence isn't necessary. Emotions make good servants, but poor masters" Ndeble interjects.

"He speaks as if our wounds were only scratches! He needs first hand experience in a third world existence. I want him to know the pain his father caused while he stood by watching millions of people suffer and die needlessly while he had the power to stop it all along! How can we believe a word he says?" Evolon announces.

"He is our way opener. And I assure you, that he will be the first to drink the purified water" Ndbele said.

All the while Saisir is looking at the floor to conceal the fact that he was fighting back tears.

"He killed my mother" he mumbles incoherently.

Pulling the .45 out Evolon flies out the chair and attacks Saisir. She has kicked him out of his chair backwards which is now overturned and has one hand wrapped around his throat with the other hand she begins to pistol whip him mercilessly until Bethlehem physically intercedes. He grabs her armed hand and pries the bloody pistol from her fingers and hands it off to Ndeble who is no longer the only calm person left in the room.

"Wait! We are about to witness the continuation of a two thousand year old struggle over who will control the world's water come to an end!" Ndeble intervenes and points to Saisir's now bloody face.

"He is here to risk his life and privilege for the benefit of all humanity. If you deny him that right then you are no better than the gatekeepers. All living things have a DNA sequence made up of the same four letters: A T C and G. The only thing that makes us different is the number and order of those letters. He comes from different numbers. You come from a different order. Close the sacred circle! Settle your quarrels, come together, understand the reality of our situation, understand that fascism is here, that people are dying who could be saved, that generations more will live poor butchered half-lives if we fail to act! Life can only be understood backwards; but it must be lived forwards! Energy is the embryo of everything. Negative energy aborts it. Positive energy raises it. We must have the patience to wait for the mud to settle in the water and the water to become clear!" Ndeble chastises his daughter.

Evolon is lifted up by her father and embraced. Saisir is still laying on the floor with his hands over his bloody face and his feet in the air.

"He killed my mother! Okay? He killed my mother!" He screams through tears and blood.

Everyone's attention returns to Saisir and begins to settle back down. Ndebele positions himself between Evolon and Saisir. Bethlehem helps Saisir up, hands him a handkerchief and a small cold pack from the first-aid kit. He picks the chair back up so that he can seat down.

"Do not be angry with the rain; it simply does not know how to fall upwards." He glares in Evolon's direction before returning to face Saisir. "Sorry, we don't have more ice." Bethlehem apologizes for more than the lack of ice. "Hope you like rainwater. The dedicated cyclist purified it." He puts another tea cup on the table.

Saisir minds his wounds. He first wipes his face and dabs the remaining clean area of the handkerchief into the first cup of water to finish the job. Then he puts the cold pack to his face and slowly sips the rainwater from the fresh tea cup before he begins.

"She was the first to drink the contaminated solution he forced me to develop. I was just a weird, rich kid, a failed chemist that knew how to make GHB at home to get the girls. May father's security advisors informed him of the growing mood of resistance and suggested that he increase the daily amount of rationed water to 50 liters per person. He rejected this as being too socialist and kind hearted. He thought it would make him appear weak by showing compassion. So he had me introduced it into the public water supply. At first, I was like hey, you know, more girls for me. But I screwed up the proper measurements, a failed chemist in true fashion I guess. I had just never undertaken such a large scale production before and I was forced to go at it alone because my father was paranoid of anyone else finding out. But he took the cup of this concentrated solution to my mother who hadn't even spoken more than three words to him in my presence most of my life let alone share her bed. I told him I couldn't be sure if it was safe so he should try watering his garden with it to monitor the results. He refused and said that he had the perfect guinea pig. I thought it was going to be one of his gardeners. They get killed every time one of his precious flowers dies. But he used my mother. The only person alive that remembered him before Global Water came to power and became the oasis of the New World" Saisir shares his most intimate secrets.

"How did it happen?" An emphatic Evolon now asks.

"She slipped into a coma and died a few weeks later. But the real horror for me is the fact that my father raped my mother every single night that she was in that coma. He said it was all an accident and that his sexual perversion was a manifestation of his undying lover for her. I knew that was bullshit. He'd just paid her back for all those years her bed was closed to him and wouldn't touch him" Saisir now takes a gulp to finish the rainwater in his tea cup and looks down at the floor as tears washes away any remaining blood on his face.

"So you do know the pain your father has caused" Evolon says softly.

"Yes I do" Saisir responds through gritted teeth.

"What was her name?" Evolon inquires.

"Cura" Saisir is surprised by the question and perceives that as the closest thing to an apology he can expect from her.

Ndeble replenishes both his and Saisir's tea cup with rainwater.

"What makes you father so cruel?" Bethlehem asks.

"My entire life, my father rarely, if ever spoke of his childhood. The one story I remember him telling me was when he was a boy, say 9 or 10, he was daydreaming looking out the window until his mother walked up and slapped the water out of his mouth. Apparently, she had been calling his name several times and he was lost in thoughts daydreaming and hadn't responded. He spoke of how that hurt him and how that was the day he realized that he hated his mother. He had to assume power so that he would never be on the receiving end of those in power" Saisir explains.

"Anyone who does not mourn the death of their mother should join her and be put to death. It is far easier to raise strong children than to repair broken men. Shall we continue Saisir please" Ndbele said.

Saisir gathers himself together. Wipes his eyes, adjusts the cold pack and sips his rainwater. He takes a very deep breath and clears his throat.

"Next you add an equal amount of salt as an enzyme cleaner. This will absorb the solution during the reverse osmosis and activated carbon filtration. But this is all a very slow process. Storage tanks are required to produce an adequate volume in a reasonable amount of time" Saisir resumes his explanation.

"And this will return the tainted water to its pure state?" Bethlehem offers a rare interjection looking up from his notebook.

"Well the term pure is somewhat ambiguous. It as different connotations to individuals in various fields. The bacteriologist is apt to regard 'pure water' as a sterile liquid, while the chemist on the other hand might well classify water pure when it possesses no mineral or organic impurities. But true pure water is likely to be found only in laboratories and even then only under ideal conditions" Saisir concludes his irrelevant discourse.

Evolon has impatiently dropped her head as the others sighed and joined her in expressing their mild disdain for Saisir's interminable exposition.

"But can we safely drink the shit?" Evolon asks.

"You don't need to have a PhD in water management, but yes of course. I am simply undoing what I have already done." Saisir explains.

"Feral cats can determine the validity of the water, I am sure" Bethlehem again interjects.

"I am quite aware of the Resistance effective use of animals to locate, drink or abandon a water source. But we must be mindful that there are only a few handfuls of water bodies in the wilderness and many are 'dirty' by human standards but wild animals must rely upon them to quench their thirst. This is due to the fact that regular consumption from the same source will help them get used to the 'dirty' water and develop an immune system that adapts and build endurance and tolerance. But this is only true when the microbial population in those water bodies are stable. If there's a sudden change in the microbial profile in that particular waterbody, then the outcomes will be deadly. However, the survivors will then pass the 'resistance' to their offspring and develop a tolerance" Saisir openly shares for full disclosure.

"Then whoever doesn't die will ensure the survival of others?" Evolon asks.

"Basically, yeah" Saisir concurs.

"Unfucking believable..." Evolon exasperates and turns directly to her father "Wait for the mud to settle in the water and the water to become clear?"

"Very well then, these are all acceptable risks. Now we must work to obtain these materials. A storage tank of such size would have to be underground" Ndeble said.

"Yes and it should be buried at least thirty-six inches below grade in order to remain ice free and discourage algae or bacteria. You do have a site for such a tank don't you?" Saisir asks.

"There are plenty of sinkholes that could be used" Evolon suggests.

"Dear god. We wouldn't have a sufficient liner to contain the water and such an open source would be easily detected. How do you expect this to work? This sounds hopeless. You don't have enough time to construct a site even if you had all the materials and manpower" Saisir surmises.

"We could simply use an abandon gas station and set up there. We can disinfect the tanks by flushing it with a mixture of baking soda and vinegar, correct?" Ndbele submits accurately.

Saisir pauses to first ponder the notion, then facially displayed his bourgeois thinking that condescendingly decided that it should be sufficient enough for the peasants before he affirmed and acknowledged "Yes. That is correct if it is made out of stainless steel or aluminum to ensure that there is no rust present and provided, of course, the mixture is prepared in the proper ratio. I would also use boiled linseed oil just to be safe. It dries fast and is non-toxic."

"Is the failed chemist prepared for success this time?" Ndbele asks.

"I do believe we learn best, from our own mistakes" Saisir replies.

"True indeed" Nbeble agrees. "I think it is safe to let you in on a little dirty secret Saisir."

Immensely intrigued to hear this revelation Saisir asks, "Oh yeah, what's that?"

"I designed the capsule program to dispose of all the bodies your father created. Which in turn produced all the fertile soil that prevented the Southside of Nineveh from starving and provided..."

"The soil for my father's gardens? That's how you knew of the water supply of my father's greenhouses?" Saisir realizes that his own father's excesses were inadvertently funding the Resistance the entire time.

Ndbele smiles slyly. "One body and a few wheelbarrows at a time. So when he killed us, we literally made him pay for it."

"Roses become compost." Bethlehem and Evolon repeating in unison publicly confirming to everyone in the room to the intimacy of their relationship.

"Amazing. You know my father is actually preparing to celebrate your demise three nights from now" Saisir adds.

"Courtesy of Canaan's unseen assistance no doubt" Evolon said.

"Wait, what? So Canaan is actually assisting in this? Well then, this might just work" Saisir says with assurance.

"Almost close, almost here" Bethlehem closes his notebook.

"With the majority of Security Forces pulled away, this will present the best opportunity to gain access to the laboratories to secure some of the materials that are needed. I must make an excuse for not attending" Saisir offers.

"No. You must go. We have all the information that we need and we cannot afford any further attention being drawn to you. You must go. Bethlehem you find a suitable location for our tanks that meet our requirements. Evolon you return Saisir after he has prepared the first tank of purified water in your presence and provided the proper ratio for the necessary disinfectants for the tanks. This is our hour of burning and nothing but light will come from these fires" Ndebele ends his instructions with an affirmation.

Everyone is now dismissed and rises in motion to exit. Ndeble reaches for the tea cup that belong to his wife. He pours himself another cup and drinks it fast. He turns the one Saisir used upside down. He walks over to the window to witness the departure of his unconventional squad. He retrieves a picture of his late wife Assata and a bottle of rum. He speaks to her as gently as he caresses the image and sips the rum from his tea cup as slowly as fingers touches her face.

"Water, whose soft architectural hands have power to cut stones and chisel shapes of grandeur in mountains. Our home is not the same, dear heart, since you were called away, there's grief and sorrow always here. Since that sad fatal day; but the hearts that loved you dearly, through our grief we ever fight. Until we meet you in your happy home... someday" Ndeble whispers to himself. He then bows his head in a prayer. "Wami odara odara wami Yemoja fun mi lowo Translation: Bring me good things, good things, Mother of Fish bring me abundance."

Evolon and Bethlehem are approaching the car with Saisir. Evolon watches him adjust the cold pack on the knot on the side of his head.

"For what it is worth, I am sorry about your mother" she offers.

"For what is is worth, I am sorry about whatever happened to your mother" he responds.

They get in the car. Evolon notices that Saisir seems distraught about more than the knot on his head.

"What's the problem pretty boy?" She asks.

"Until you lose something, you don't recognize its value. I am being forced to question the foundational axiom that has driven my entire operating system. I've just now realized that I am committing sexual suicide here" he confesses.

"I am sure you will find new interests" Bethlehem offers as he pulls the car away.

"Really? You think so?" Saisir seems mildly excited by the notion of that thought.

"Yeah. It's called masturbation" Evolon turns around to laugh at his pain.

"The death of a dream" Saisir sorrowfully and slowly shakes his head.

"This is only the beginning. A beginning we have never seen before. The death of nothing. The birth of something. Hard times have a way of making us more aware of our creative skills that would remain dormant during good times" the reflective Bethlehem closes the conversation as the car slowly disappears into the night and Ndeble's unconventional squad continues the remainder of the ride in silence.

CHAPTER 10
THE PALACE

Believing that the Resistance has been put down, Nimrod has thrown a lavish affair at his opulent palace to solidify his power and reconfirm his absolute fascist authority. This was necessary in order to satisfy any doubts from the corrupt members of the Natural Resource Defense Council that is a paper tiger and a clandestinely veiled organization that was supposed to represent the will of the people but was handsomely compensated to betray them. And of course, the members of the Global Water Corporation that actually held the true power and reaped the lion's share of water profits with Nimrod as the head.

Outside, all the obese attendees, who are early to arrive, are first greeted by crowds of thirty protesters beyond the gates, until Canaan is summoned to put down the disturbance in a most unusual way. Since the beginning of time we have all been told to be wary of wolves in sheep clothing. But they failed to warn us that their words would be even more dangerous than their teeth.

The rebellious crowds of thirsty protesters are chanting "Water Justice! People before profit! Supply from the sky! More Water! More Life!" All in complete unison.

Surprisingly, Canaan himself appears with a small security force and receives the silence his reputation deserves when he is recognized and invokes a mighty hurricane of emotions and muted debates among the group with fearing the worst but reassured they wouldn't be slaughtered in plan view of the posh Palace's illustrious attendees. He is provided a microphone to a large bull horn on a Security Forces vehicle. He addresses his startled and attentive audience who are lead by a few that have been embolden by the Resistance's untainted water distribution.

"My dear and lowly citizens of Nineveh! We greet you! I have wonderful news! I have been summoned here to invite all of you unto the Palace grounds of Nimrod. So please, join us all for the feast of your lives and enjoy all the richness that this spectacular event has to offer. We embrace you! An extravagant lawn party has just been organized in honor of your long struggle and suffering. The Resistance is now over. If there is anyone amongst you that has a list of their grievances that needs to be heard, I will take it to the Natural Resource Defense Council myself personally. Public opinion is everything. It is not enough to just stand up. You must now step forward to speak truth to power, we have felt your pain and we want to hear from you. Global Water is now committed to a more equitable redistribution of its water and its wealth! Please, come! Join us! We welcome you!" Canaan now concludes his disingenuous but effective monologue.

Canaan's sweet sugary approach successfully muted the chants and tempered most of the crowd's righteous indignations. All but a few were enticed into the gates of the Palace to enjoy the wool of the sheep covering the wolves. The few that refused saw the teeth of the same wolves as they were arrested beyond the purview of their seduced comrades. The party crashers were treated relatively well and provided an outdoor dinner buffet, alcohol and all the tainted water they could possibly carry. This made them quite pacified and content, but they were restricted to the lawn party only on the grounds farthest from the Palace clearly long out the sight of most of the guests still arriving. Canaan is handed a list of grievances from the boldest of the desperate and hopeful which are casually discarded as soon as he is out of the horizon of their sight.

All the oppressive systems of the history of the entire world dares not create the basis for working towards a more equitable society for it would lead to a most disastrous disruption of their own society and inescapable overthrow of their own privileges and status. At least that is what conventional wisdom says and an accurate view history has shown us. So he directs his Security Force to secure the perimeter and shut off all the timed sprinkler systems.

Inside the grand Palace in the center of the large glorious ballroom stands a magnificent twenty-five foot water fountain, aquariums in the walls and thousands of freshly cut ornamental flowers fresh from Nimrod's bloodied Victorian Glass greenhouse collection. Most of the attendees are older than the now pacified and full protesters hidden from view outside and are obese except for the few party girls allowed in attendance. Most are shareholders in the Global Water Corporation, members of the Natural Resource Defense Council, International Monetary Fund, World Bank, unidentified members of the Bilderberg Group or numerous other dedicated sycophants that functioned as the monsters in little Saisir's nightmares poured into the governorate of Nineveh and filled the Palace. Nimrod quietly enters the ballroom and is exchanging pleasantries while holding court in a small circle of knowledge when he's greeted.

"I must say Nimrod, that even for the richest man in Babylon, this is clearly the most exquisite affair I have ever attended at this splendid Palace. Well worth the Hyperloop ride from the Western Provinces. One would think he was actually at the World Water Forum in Kyoto or even the Buckingham Palace before the fall of the Monarchy" the first attendee laments.

"By the leaves of this gathering, I must confess, that I am well compensated for my time being shared with people I don't like." Nimrod gestures out the windows to indicate all the seduced former protesters outside, but this is only to politely cloak the double entendre that also targets his other intentions standing before him. "But thank you. You are far too kind." Nimrod's stoic face concludes with a forced grin.

"Oh no sir my lord. It is you who's far, far, too kind, allowing ordinary people to enjoy an evening of luxury rather than having them all arrested and thrown into the dungeons where they belong. Or better yet, decomposing in a capsule to create wheelbarrows of soil for your private gardens.

Is this some act of charity? An effort to disrupt the nature of things?" The second attendee sarcastically comments.

"Perhaps it's piety, considering the corruption of his son's addiction to the commons and their filth. These people still believe, despite all the kilo years of the millennia, that the Bible is a history book like dinosaurs never even existed" the third attendee adds sparking a round of robust laughter.

"But I must admit to you that your supposed performance of political theatre consuming tainted water from the public supply was indeed a successful publicity stunt." The first attendee continues to interject his attack.

"And if I may dare to be so bold, some could even go as far to suggest that Nimrod is indeed forbearing and being uncharacteristically merciful in his newly found pathos" the third attendee finishes the round of soft combat of derision.

The last comment garners more mildly restrained laughter amongst those in the circle of the group that is quickly suppressed when Nimrod begins to speak.

"I must assure you that my well deserved reputation is still very much intact. It is merely a question of credibility of both labor and elite. Labor's choice is obviously between confrontation and that of non-confrontation. While the elite's choice is solely between distributional and non-distributional policies which are influenced by the perceptions of all the other groups commitment to either enforce or challenge whichever policy is adopted. However, wars are costly and no longer profitable like they were when most of the world was still a litigious society and had enough water to last them all year and were deceived by their abundance. The Water Crisis has caused the masses of people to focus. Whose need of our products is the source of all our wealth. If they are not lulled into some level of complacency in regards to our water holding frog policies of stakeholder capitalism; well then neither I nor your counsel have done our job to manufacture consent.

If the real battle in this nation state and in the world were revealed that it is no longer the Right or the Left, but in fact the People vs the Oligarchy in the weaponization of water, then I assure you our privileged position's days would be numbered. No oppressed people will fight and endure without the promise of something better than a mere change of masters. Let's not forget that the great Nikola Tesla's Wardeclyffe Tower was intended to transmit electricity wirelessly to the world. But after it was constructed, his funder J.P. Morgan discovered that transmitting energy to the entire world could not be commodified profitably at all under this system and to make matters worst, Tesla intended to free the masses from their energy dependent debt by providing it at no cost. Well, that tower was quickly and quietly destroyed. And people paid electric bills for centuries. Much like our lucrative requisition of the water supply was precipitated by a crisis that enabled us to further enrich ourselves.

All fueled by our collective greed and enforced by a necessary level of brutality. But we must not be too greedy nor too brutal. Maintaining power is just like holding an egg. Too much force and you break it. Not enough force, you drop it. Good leadership requires that people do what you want them to do because they want to. We must continue to afford the lower class some level of a fallacy of hope in order to continue our policy of benign neglect. Just like all the poor souls outside. Without hope, people are too dangerous. This is what fueled the Resisters. But the plant can grow no larger than the flower pot we design that contains them. Those who are conquered always want to imitate the conqueror in his characteristics. That is our true advantage.

We have an agreement with these people. They can say what they want and we can do what we want. Need I remind you in these monetary circles that each of your contracts represent 100 acre meters of water and those contracts will not be financially settled if the buyers of those contracts don't hold on through the required expiration. Unless they choose to be greeted by a delivery of millions of liters of water to sell on a flooded market literally and figuratively. Whose thirst has been quenched by the rain or another rebellion. Therefore, you should all pray to all our colonizing ancestors for our continued success rather than rejoice in my alleged downfall, especially with the Sword of Damocles hanging over your heads. Since the greatest threats to your health and wealth is our political hyponatremia and my rage. You can rest assure that whether by conquest or consent, the public has been reduced to its proper state of apathy and obedience. Now if you would excuse me, I have a celebration of the Resistance that we just put down to toast to" Nimrod abruptly concludes.

Nimrod continues on his way to proceed to ascend the crystal stairs up to the illustriously elevated glass podium behind a large colorful bouquet of his prized hydrangea flowers and the deadly foxglove plant in full bloom as a kind of botanical display of war and peace. He addresses those in attendance as well as an even larger listening audience via Security Force speakers posted on light poles throughout the city-state of Nineveh, State Radio and other digital broadcasts distributed to the remaining world. The arrival of his presence is greeted by a resounding round of applause by enthusiastic, but insincere, fat bourgeois hands. Cameras flash and champagne glasses go high in the air.

"Honorable citizens of the great city-state of Nineveh! On behalf of the Natural Resource Defense Council, the IMF, the World Bank and the Global Water Corporation we welcome all of you! We come to you now through a bleak reality that until most recently seemed even grimmer. We have all witnessed an uprising that threatened our peace and defied law and order with an utter disregard to both life and private property. These benighted agent provocateurs who led this brutal Resistance were all foreign anarchists here to incite the law abiding lumpen proletariats of this city state and now have all been brought to justice" Nimrod said as he's interrupted by thunderous applause. He begins to gently cough as if to clear his throat. He looks around the podium and asks for a glass of water. He is quickly but mistakenly presented with a flute of champagne from a liveried servant that unfortunately ruins yet another moment of opportunity for his political theatre.

"As some of you know, these impertinent terrorists even kidnapped my own beloved son. Once we were able to negotiate his safe return he had to then endure several weeks of isolation in the dungeons of Nineveh simply to ensure his welfare and protection until the rebellion was put down. If it were not for the complete dedication of our elite Security Forces determined to preserve our way of life and protect our society and liberty, there wouldn't be any cause of celebration here today, especially if I had lost my only child" Nimrod raises his champagne flute to his son as the enthralled audience does the same in silence. Saisir is seen reluctantly joining the toast with his glass barely raised to his shoulder level with a tight grin and no teeth shown as his free hand uncomfortably begins to adjust the tie around his neck while he stands in the close proximity of several adoring obese women who are clearly enjoying the pleasure of his company too much to his cloaked disdain.

Nimrod continues, "We pay tribute to the many lives that were sacrificed to bring down this Resistance and restore law and order to our beloved city state. Now let's have a moment of silence for all the lives lost on behalf of our brave and dedicated

Security Forces..." He lowers his head and all the attendees and even the pacified protesters outside follow suit except for those of Canaan and Saisir in the Palace who directly catch each other eyes and lock momentarily. That brief moment of silence is ended when more champagne bottles begin to pop.

"For a time, many worried about the direction of our world. They worried about our culture where only the physically or materially dominant have the sole right to speak. Anything less than victory is unfit for freemen and only worthy of slaves; it would be a very flagrant outrage upon common sense and propriety. So we urge all those in the sound of my voice to release all their thoughts of lack and limitation as we are now renewed in mind body and spirit. And as as act of charity and goodwill to the faithful we have increased the government water rations and have even opened our gates for those least of us to join in our triumph and celebration. From the glaciers of the Arctic to the Blue Nile of the Sudan; we bring you what the world thirsts for..." the entire audience shouts in unison "Global Water!"

"Now let us all live the highest vision of what is possible!" He concludes to more thunderous applause and finishes the champagne left in his flute and flashes deadly eyes to the attendant that missed his water cue and mistakenly handed it to him while he replenished his glass with shaking hands. Nimrod is a subtle beast. He proves once and for all, that there are more ruthless people in business than there are in the streets. He then forces him to retrieve some water in the vase containing the same large display of foxglove plants and demands that he drink it while he watched him with retribution. Thereby, committing an insidious act of murder in plane sight unbeknownst to anyone but that of the victim. But unbeknownst to the monstrous murderer at the pinnacle of his power, it proved to be his last victim.

CHAPTER 11

HER WATER BREAKS

During Nimrod's speech the Resisters are hard at work preparing massive amounts of untainted water. Time passes as the Resister's numbers multiply a hundred fold. Not quite the number of sunfish eggs that Nimrod feared would reach maturity, but significant enough to challenge effectively with the assistance of betrayal's pretty face to destabilize the Persian rugs beneath the foundation of his empire. The pillars of power were now as shaky as the lemonade tray in the trembling hands of Tiki's immobilized body when he witnessed the brutal murder of Siemele. The Resister's were ready, but not prepared. The Security Forces were prepared, but not ready. Eventually, they are contacted by Canaan as to the best opportune time to storm the palace grounds as the majority of the security forces were to be preoccupied by a military exercise.

Even with the reduced Security Forces, an entire battalion was on duty patrolling the ground and manning their posts surrounding the Palace with another dedicated Regiment on standby. Diversions were created to draw the first squad from the gates and out into the open as Canaan's invaluable assistance provided the codes to scramble their communication system that significantly delayed the battalion's response time so that they couldn't rally a fully proper defense and didn't even realize they were actually under attack until it was too late with a full platoon nearly decimated before the first Resister fell.

In life, there are sometimes fault lines and power shifts. There are tales of mothers imbued with supernatural strength in defense of their children. Similarly, bravery and fear can too, trade places despite the vessels that carry it. Under normal circumstances, if David challenged Goliath outright without his sling shot, all would have been lost. However, put the giant Goliath in bed with David's wife that he loved more than anything else in the world and we'll see who's afraid when David walks into the room.

A power shift was occurring in the Palace. Some Security Forces were abandoning their post. The fear that they had instilled into the masses had given them a false sense of power. It was this fear that ruled the people. It was their inability to recognize that the greatest power was convincing people that they didn't have any was what maintained that fear. Now, fear was trading places. However, despite the well executed plan and the Resister's superior position and the moral authority of their emotionally motivated guerrilla company swinging for the fence, the brawny, beautiful and brilliant Bethlehem falls to a fusillade of gun fire a few steps away from Evolon who rushes to his side immediately after eliminating the threat. He is mortally wounded. She takes him in her arms under cover while their guerrilla company continues to engage and the cacophony of battle seems to fade.

"There is nothing more exhilarating than being shot at and missed. Getting shot at never bothered me. But getting hit will shake you up." Bethlehem whispers.

"Bullets look a lot better when they ain't coming at you" Laughing, crying, rocking her body back and forth Evolon whispers back with a kiss as she cradles his head in her lap.

"Bethlehem..." she begins.

"my fire... my light... the jasmine smearing around its bruised secrets, terrifying love, pure soft hands, pure peace into my eyes and sun into my senses. O love, how quickly you built a sweet firmness where

the wounds had been: You fought off the talons and claws, and now we stand as single life before the world. That's how it was, is and will be my wild sweet love, till time signals us with the day's last flowers. Then there will be no you, no light and yet beyond the earth, beyond its shadowy dark, the splendor of our love will be alive."

He smiles "Wow.. that was almost beautiful. Did you write that?" Bethlehem whispers again with blood showing in his teeth.

"No... it's Neruda's XXIII. It is the only poem I have ever committed to memory. I was going to recite it to you when this battle was over and I could I tell you I was pregnant" Evolon answers him while wiping her own tears that have fallen upon his face.

"They have destroyed our ancestors and tortured our families, but we have planted a garden. Let your life do the singing" he says.

"Thank you for meaning so much to my father and to us" she responds while placing her hand upon his.

Bethlehem smiles faintly and utters his last words while touching her stomach with the palm of his left hand while caressing her face with his right, "If we must die, let us nobly die, so that our precious blood may not be shed in vain; then even the monsters we defy shall be constrained to honor us though dead. Traveling is searching my love. Home is what you have found. Remember, roses become compost and words never die. Please plant a tree for me with the barrel of my black fertile soil."

"Black is the center of everything. Telling the story of what happened. I promise..." Evolon commits.

He dies in her arms in the bright sunshine with an outdoor marble staircase for cover while the sounds of the war drums of the gun battle continues to play. When Evolon finally releases him she realizes his book of numbers is now in her bloodied hands. Rage returns to her grieving heart like two disagreeable objects that cannot occupy the same place at the same time. She lays Bethlehem's body against the staircase sitting upright and closes his eyes with a kiss. She covers his body with her jacket. She reloads and rises to her feet. Her fallen tears no longer moistens the ground like melting ice watering an orchid that will survive but may never bloom again.

After overpowering the remaining guards and with Saisir as a guide, Evolon's squad are still in search of Nimrod and prepared to fight until the last person falls.

"Where is he?" Evolon exclaims after they searched all the rooms in the palace. "Could he have escaped?"

"No. He must be in the pool. Since all this began, he has suffered from insomnia and apparently his sleeping pills work best on water." Saisir leads the way to the pool.

Nimrod, who has been completely oblivious to the ensuing battle, is basking in the sunshine on a float in his salt water pool with noise cancelling headphones on enjoying the affects of the sleeping pills.

He is only alerted to their presence not when their shadows begin to block his sunlight from the terrace over looking the olympic size swimming pool, but when he is startled out of his sleep when Evolon shoots his float and realizes that she now has an electrical device that she is threatening to drop into the water when she holds it high over head.

"What is the meaning of this?" Nimrods says while alerting his Security Forces that never responds. "What do you want?"

"To turn your sick soul inside out so the world can watch you die!" Screams Evolon.

"Saisir, my beloved gentle son! Please put a stop to this!" Nimrod begs.

"This is the world you have made for yourself. Now drown in it." Saisir replies.

"So you are carrying water for the Resistance now? This is how I finally get to see your strength? Strong as the wood from an olive tree, but still sensitive to the outside elements and insects! Do you know why wicked men are prosperous and brutal men succeed? Do you? Because there is no profit to be made in peace! Or in saving the planet! Only in controlled destruction. And that has always been true since the beginning of time! So you will never have the utopia you want! There will always be a war going on and plenty of men willing to kill for profit. You should show sympathy to the devil and anger towards god!" Nimrod screams.

"You continue to believe that you have something to teach the world without ever learning something from it is beyond arrogance. It is fascist supremacy! You don't know the difference between knowledge and understanding or even right or wrong. And for that, you have my deepest sympathies." Saisir says.

"Your mother's womb should have been your grave! She cried the day you were born!" Nimrod barks.

"I cried the day she fell into that coma and died! Did you? Now hang on to your rosary beads motherfucker!

"Death is preferable to disgrace!" Nimrod screams.

He snatches the electrical device that Evolon was holding and drops it into the swimming pool causing Nimrod to be electrocuted.

They look down upon his body floating face down.

"What a waste." Evolon said.

"It had to be done." Saisir said.

"I was talking about the water. I see you've gone through some funky changes." Evolon quips.

Canaan and the Regiment of Security Forces loyal to him arrive on the scene. They face off and surround the remaining guerrilla company of Resisters outnumbering them. Both he and Evolon signal not to fire.

"Well, well, well this is a pleasant surprise. I didn't know you had it in you Saisir. It seems I was wrong about you. Looks like in your transmutation, you can remain a very malleable character and still turn a lady bug blue after all." Canaan said.

"Everyday is a pleasant surprise if it's a good day; a bad day is the same old shit." Evolon said still standing on guard.

Canaan smiles and walks to the edge of the terrace to look over. He sees Nimrod's dead body in its watery grave and smiles even more broadly.

"Apparently, blood is not thicker than the water that divides us. I see we are done here." Canaan said.

"Are we done or just beginning to start Canaan?" Evolon responds defensively as more Resisters join her and make the situation even more tense.

"Steel against steel makes for a sharper blade my dear, but let's give peace a chance first, shall we? I assure you, it is a lot cheaper than the price of one cowrie." Canaan replies calmly.

He now announces to all those in attendance.

"I hereby relinquish all control of Global Water to Saisir for him to do as he sees fit. The Natural Defense Council will now be controlled by the leaders of the Resistance. Take all stake holders into custody." Canaan states.

"Is that a good sign that somebody actually cares?" Evolon asks in amazement.

"Oh contraire my dear. This is as far as we're going to go. Don't let the smooth taste fool you. I am far from a benevolent humanitarian. The truth has many enemies. Lies have many friends. I am still very much a capitalist and a firm believer in oligarchy. And as such, I will continue to provide for those who can afford to pay for my services. With untainted water now returning to the hands of the masses, the upper class will now need new alternatives to differentiate themselves from the lumpen proletariats and confirm their superior social status." Canaan explains.

"What are you proposing to do Canaan?" Saisir drills him.

"Oxygen bars my boy. Your dearly departed father was right. There is no profit in peace. Why do you think I made a career in the military? While you were busy destroying one world order, I was contending to build another." Canaan says with a big smile.

"So now with the lack of want from thirst, we must now be choked by the likes of you?" Evolon exclaims in frustration.

"From the sweat of our brows to the vapors of our breath" Saisir adds.

"When you pray for rain, you got to deal with the mud too. Saisir's brokenness to boldness and parricide has merely assassinated a tyrant and open the floodgates as you wished. It has not however, destroyed structural classism or all the dystopian aspects of our society. While water may no longer be a commodity, there are still levels to the quality and the same applies to the air. Some carry a foul stench and some are fresh. Oxygen bars are springing up all around the world like coffee shops in places where high levels of pollution have produced widespread desire for a breath of fresh air. I did not create this demand for freedom from Nineveh's urine stenched streets. I am simply profiting from patrons who are as willing to spend money for a breath of fresh air as they are on alcohol, women or water." Canaan directs each of his selected vices to the appropriate vessels before he continues. "Even the kindest person to every walk on this earth was a villain in someone's story. So we shall be opening up a new mine, the wealth of which has not yet been explored. As the first occupants of this mine, it will be our privilege to select and exploit the best reactant in cellular respiration. So, as you say from, de Coeur, 'French translation: the heart' there is no love over here, time's a wasting, let the bloody peace begin! Auvoir." Nimrod and his loyal Security Forces exits briskly and gracefully, but without ever turning their backs.

"The love is sometimes fake, but the hate is always real. Never have so few taken so much from so many for so long." Evolon surmises watching them make their exit.

"And he who guardeth his tongue guardeth his life." Saisir speaks as if talking to himself before turning to look directly at her. "For many years, I never said how I feel or even believed what I said. But hey, I'm sorry about your friend, Bethlehem." Saisir offers.

She exhales and turns around to face him. "Thank you. I'm sorry I am not able to say the same about your father" Evolon replies and reaches to hold his hand to finally close the sacred circle. "This present moment used to be the unimaginable future. You didn't have to do what you did, but you did. For that, I thank you."

They look down from the terrace overlooking Nimrod's watery grave as his lifelessly body floats face down.

"We are fortunate to be where we are so therefore we are obligated to help others. I thank you for waking me up to that. Olukun ba wa o" translation: Spirit of the Ocean save us. Saisir spits in the pool.

"We will touch lives that haven't even been born yet. Bas wa Orisha Ba wo o oe." Translation: Save us Spirit save us all. Evolon spits in the pool too.

Aqua, the pet Koala Bear, comes down from one of the eucalyptus trees as on cue now that all the commotion has subsided. He climbs on to Nimrod's favorite round patio daybed seemingly joining the group to watch a new sunset.

They all watch the sun set together as Evolon and Saisir continue to hold hands as tightly as if their lives depended on the bond not ever breaking. It was not a bond of love, but as if a bond of two strangers forced together by life and dire circumstances joining hands before leaping from a burning building they could not safely escape from.

Without removing her eyes from gazing at the setting sun Evolon asks Saisir a question. "Saisir, let me ask you something. Is a piano a stringed instrument or a percussion instrument?"

Saisir looks in astonishment "What?"

AFTERWORD

Let us understand this: supply comes form the sky. So let us apply the understanding, that in order to meet demand, we need to harvest the rain. Not dam a river and block its flow. Not boost water out of aquifers like giant straws in the ground and suck the earth dry and create a sunken place for the world. We must approach old problems with a renewed mind. Not build canals or pipelines. But merely harvest the rain. If nothing is put back in, it will eventually run out. Those in charge of our planet are either corrupt or guilty of gross mismanagement of the world's natural resources and environmental neglect and pillage. It is a false hope that these same governments and policy makers will make a renewed commitment to come to grips with the impending international water crisis and conflicts in a geological blink of an eye. What's worse is that the West has been on a path of greed and destruction since its inception. So the irony is not lost on the bigger difficulty that in the rich West, water is largely taken for granted. And as more nations develop their economies, the need for water will only increase if they continue to imitate the unsustainable model of the West. And while the life-threatening demand for this precious natural resource increases, the supply is likely to remain unchanged, drastically increasing the chances for more armed conflict over water.

We don't have to look into the future for these violent conflicts. We can simply go back to 1999 in Cochabamba, Bolivia for a modern water war. Then President Hugo Banzer, a dictator supported by the West, allowed the privatization of the water. The Bechtel corporation, that built the Hoover Dam and got the contract along with Haliburton to reap the spoils of rebuilding Iraq after it was destroyed by the West, was the sole bidder to win the water rights contract that was coerced by the World Bank. Overnight the average rate increase was over 50%. In addition, Bechtel had a stipulation in their contract that guaranteed a 16% return on their investments. It was theft.

People stopped paying their water bills. Bechtel started cutting off water. People started protesting. A General Strike was called and shutdown the city for two days demanding that the water contract be rolled back. The government then outlawed protesting. They called in police from around the country because the local police wouldn't fire on the crowds so the outside police started shooting, first with rubber bullets and then live ammunition.

> *"We have always repeated those slogans 'Death to the World Bank' 'death to the IMF.' 'Down with Yan-kee Imperialism.' But I believe that it is the first time that the people understood in a direct way how the policies of the World Bank, Free Trade, Free Marketsis putting us at such a disadvantage among the most powerful countries."*
>
> –Oscar Olivera

Then the ultimate battle ensued. The people refused to backdown until the water contracts were cancelled. Martial law was declared. The prisons were so filled that they took planes to fly people to the jungle to detain them. Some people went missing. The government cut power off to take out TV and Radio stations from reporting. But in a modern day David and Goliath, the people defeated an army with sling shots and fearless determination for water is life. Four months of struggle and the privatization was untenable. Bechtel cancelled the contracts and left the country. But the empire strikes back. Bechtel then sued Bolivia for $50 million for the lost of future profits in a Trade Tribunal at the World Bank who coerced the "trade" in the first place.

Obviously, the proceedings were done in private. So a global campaign was launched to hang the water revolt around the neck of Bechtel who later settled the case for a token payment of thirty cents. This later led to the rise of Evo Morales, the very first indigenous President of Bolivia. But even now, the water war still continues. For what good does it make if the water pipes are under the control of the people when the glaciers from the surrounding mountains have melted and no water no longer flows through the pipes? These frozen reservoirs that provided the water have melted due to climate change.

The way we live on this planet does not work. We are engaged in theft. We are stealing from the children that follow in the future. We have a rendezvous with destiny. We need an informed Democracy and to believe we have the power to act. We must come to realize that all of our social problems have historical and psychological causes and therefore require iconoclastic solutions to challenge the institutions of inequity from Wall Street to Water Barons to the Military Industrial Complex. We must end the constant dissociation with ancestral knowledge and customs that have converted personal gardens to cabinets filled with pharmaceutical drugs. What we see now is a mere imitation of life. No more trash clogged drains, paved flood plains and deforestation. No more water bankruptcy with sprinklers watering lawns and golf courses in deserts next to to dry river beds. No more consumed drugs polluting the water and our waste posing threats undetected by current testing methods. No more Jackson, Mississippis being denied water after being defrauded by the government. No more Detroit or Flint Water Crisis near the largest body of fresh water in the world! No more thousands of daily deaths due to the lack of access to clean drinking water around the world. No more hypoxic dead zones in the Gulf Coast of Mexico the size of the State of New Jersey with oxygen levels so low that it can't support any aquatic life. Or sinking places like Mexico City. This is a confession of wishful thinking, but there must be communication with the natural world with earth and man.

During the wet years we must never forget the dry years. We must all become water conservers and put on our seatbelts, wear our helmets, regularly monitor what we not only put into our bodies, but also the earth. And finally, we must release all our fears and our natural tendency to avoid confronting danger head on at all cost and deal with the disturbing confidence of sincere ignorance and the conscientious stupidity of the West that is threatening the entire planet. Otherwise, the two thousand year-old struggle over who will control the earth's scarce water resources will continue. The borders of this new universe are still unclear, and they are constantly being redefined. But the laws of nature never change. Water is not a commodity. Water is life. In the wrong hands, water is a weapon. Don't waste it. Protect it. Fight those who steal it. People may not care about melting glaciers but they will care about conflicts. Bloodless waiting for justice goes against all the evidence history has taught us. Otherwise, we are all frogs on this planet being boiled slowly. There is no problem we are unable to resolve. Go enjoy the sunset and get ready for the sunrise.

We must realize that our future lies chiefly in our own hands.

—Paul Robeson

ABOUT THE AUTHOR

Kymone Freeman is an activist, award winning playwright, filmmaker and co-founder of We Act Radio, a full service media production company that uses disruption as a business model since 2011 in DC. He was a recipient of the 2022 Changemaker Award from the Catalogue of Philanthropy. He founded the Black L.U.V. Festival in 1997. He majored in Communications at UDC. He is the subject of one chapter of the book Beat of A Different Drum: The Untold Stories of African Americans Forging Their Own Paths in Work and Life. Freeman has appeared on local, national and international TV around the world. He has been a contributing writer to Washington Post, Ebony Magazine and several on-line publications. He is a board member of the Douglass Community Land Trust. He was part of international delegations to Cuba, Venezuela, Ghana and a summer long leadership conference in Nairobi, Kenya. He produced the Fresh Prince of Anacostia for the PBS Filmfest, a short film on on the iconic abolitionist John Brown and the Public Media Journalists Association award winning commentary "Lion and the Map" produced as an animation. His first theatrical production "Prison Poetry" won the Larry Neal Award for Drama w/ a sold-out performance at the Historic Lincoln Theatre and headlined the Hip Hop Theatre Festival. His recent stage production "The Night Michael Jackson Died" that puts the spot light on US / Cuba relations was the first theatrical performance held at the Hamilton Live in DC and appeared in NYC at the historic SOB's. Nineveh, a screenplay originally written in 2007, is his first novel.

BOOK CLUB QUESTIONS

1. What were the power dynamics in the economical exploitation of natural resources?

2. How did Evolon's family and Saisir's family resemble and differ?

3. Which character came the farthest in self-improvement?

4. Where did you see mental health play a role?

5. What was the biggest surprise for you in the story?

6. What were the common failures of both Nimrod and Ndbele?

7. Can this story serve to empower women?

8. Does this story make you optimistic or pessimistic about the future?

9. What is the connection between the body of man and the planet earth?

10. If truth is stranger than fiction, can fiction be effectively used to tell the truth?

For Bulk Orders,
please email *staff@ninevehnovel.com*

CPSIA information can be obtained
at www.ICGtesting.com
Printed in the USA
JSHW071933100323
38804JS00003B/6